HOW SHOULD AMERICA'S WILDERNESS BE MANAGED?

HOW SHOULD AMERICA'S WILDERNESS BE MANAGED?

Other books in the At Issue series:

HOW SHOULD AMERICA'S WILDERNESS BE MANAGED?

Stuart A. Kallen, *Book Editor*

Bruce Glassman, *Vice President*
Bonnie Szumski, *Publisher*
Helen Cothran, *Managing Editor*

THOMSON
* ™
GALE

San Diego • Detroit • New York • San Francisco • Cleveland
New Haven, Conn. • Waterville, Maine • London • Munich

THOMSON

™

GALE

LIBRARY OF CONGRESS CATALOGING-IN-PUBLICATION DATA

How should America's wilderness be managed? / Stuart A. Kallen, book editor.
    p. cm. — (At issue)
Includes bibliographical references and index.
ISBN 0-7377-2384-X (lib. : alk. paper) — ISBN 0-7377-2385-8 (pbk. : alk. paper)
    1. Wilderness areas—United States—Management. 2. Nature—Effect of
human beings on—United States. 3. Natural resources—United States—
Environmental aspects. I. Kallen, Stuart A., 1955– . II. At issue (San Diego, Calif.)
QH76.H69 2005
333.78'2'0973—dc22   2004042494

Contents

Introduction

People have been managing the American wilderness for thousands of years. Early Native Americans burned undergrowth in some forests to benefit hunters. They planted hillsides with medicinal herbs and diverted streams to irrigate corn, beans, and other crops. The natural world was held sacred by this relatively small population, however, and most of the American wilderness remained untouched by human hands.

When millions of people came to America from Europe during the eighteenth and nineteenth centuries, they brought a different concept of wilderness with them. They believed that the virgin American wilderness offered an endless bounty of useful game animals, trees, coal, gold, oil, and other resources that could be exploited for great wealth.

The idea of managing the wilderness would have been an odd notion in this era. The American wilderness was largely regarded as a commodity; natural resources were to be utilized for the personal gain of a few and the progress of society as a whole. In the process wild animals were hunted to extinction, millions of acres of forests were leveled, and waterways were dammed, drained, or plowed into farm fields. Oil, coal, gold, silver, and a host of other minerals were wrested from the ground. Little regard was given to the natural balance of the ecosystems that produced these resources.

By the early twentieth century, attitudes were beginning to change. The wholesale slaughter of the buffalo had reduced the once mighty herd from tens of millions to about four hundred. The eastern hardwood forests had fallen, many species of birds were tottering on the edge of extinction, and vast tracts of wild California had been destroyed by gold hunters.

The idea of setting aside wilderness areas for conservation and public enjoyment began in 1864 when Congress donated Yosemite Valley to the state of California for preservation as a park. Eight years later, Congress set aside the Yellowstone area of Wyoming and Montana as a public park for the benefit of all Americans. Other national parks were soon added, including Sequoia in California, Mount Rainier in Washington, Crater Lake in Oregon, and Glacier in Montana. The idealistic impulse to preserve nature was often joined by the desire to make money. For example, western railroads lobbied for many of the early parks to boost their tourist business. These companies also built grand rustic hotels in the parks—often in environmentally sensitive areas. Ever since that time, business interests and wilderness management have been joined together—sometimes to the advantage of both, sometimes in conflict with one another.

Today, America's fifty-four national parks remain largely untouched by loggers, ranchers, miners, and others. About half of the acreage in the parks is designated as wilderness. In these areas all industrial activity is banned, motorized vehicles are prohibited, and a limited number of overnight hikers are allowed to visit each week. These areas are managed to meet the requirements of the Wilderness Act, passed by Congress in 1964, which reads:

> A wilderness, in contrast with those areas where man and his own works dominate the landscape, is hereby recognized as an area where the earth and its community of life are un-trammeled by man, where man himself is a visitor who does not remain. An . . . area of undeveloped Federal land retain-ing its primeval character and influence, without permanent improvements or human habitation, which is protected and managed so as to preserve its natural conditions.

There are 663 areas in the United States designated as wilderness by the government—about 35 million acres total. These areas include por-tions of the national parks as well as other regions deemed sensitive. They are managed by the National Park Service, the U.S. Forest Service, and other federal agencies. While these areas are protected, there is contro-versy over their management. Some areas are being "loved to death"; that is, they are flooded with crowds of visitors who create traffic jams on nearby roads, disturb wildlife, and leave behind tons of garbage. Some ar-eas are also threatened by nearby development, where logging, oil explo-ration, air pollution, homebuilding, and off-road vehicle use threatens the character of the wilderness.

Perhaps the greatest conflict in land management is over wild areas that do not have official federal wilderness protection. These wilderness areas are managed by a host of agencies including the National Forest Ser-vice, the Bureau of Land Management, the Fish and Wildlife Service, and others. The Forest Service controls the largest amount of territory, man-aging 191 million acres of national forestland in the United States—8.5 percent of the country's landmass. About 95 million acres remain road-less. These areas are subject to the agency's congressional mandate that directs the service to manage forests for multiple uses, including timber, gas and oil exploration, recreation, and wildlife.

Like most other issues involving the government in recent years, the actions of the Forest Service and other agencies are highly politicized. Land management issues are especially divisive as decisions made by gov-ernment workers affect the livelihoods of fishermen, ranchers, loggers, oil and gas workers, and those in the tourist industry.

There are also heated battles among citizens who utilize national forests for fun. Hikers, backpackers, skiers, horseback riders, canoe pad-dlers, and environmentalists want to enjoy unspoiled areas where they can find peace, solace, and relaxation. Those who ride motorcycles, snowmo-biles, all-terrain, and other off-road vehicles want to roar through the wilderness testing their driving skills and the endurance of their machines.

With so many people competing for a shrinking wilderness, conflicts over management of these areas are rarely settled for long. No sooner does the government designate an area as wilderness than industry groups and land owners initiate lawsuits challenging the wilderness des-ignation. Conversely, when the Forest Service opens an area to logging, drilling, or mining, environmentalists sue to stop the projects.

These issues are also affected by politics. Land management issues can change overnight when one political party takes over from another. For example, when Democrat Bill Clinton was president, he had the backing of many national environmental organizations. Clinton set aside huge areas of wilderness for protection from the destructive effects of road building. When Republican George W. Bush replaced Clinton in 2000, he began reversing the roadless rules. Critics claimed Bush was simply attempting to please his political donors in the oil, gas, and logging businesses.

Politics also affect the culture of the federal agencies that manage the wilderness. Clinton appointed a renowned environmentalist, Bruce Babbitt, to head the Department of the Interior, which oversees the Forest Service, the Park Service, and other agencies. During Babbitt's tenure, the Department of Interior enacted greater protective measures for old-growth forests, endangered species, and wilderness areas while focusing less on the rights of miners, ranchers, loggers, and landowners to use those areas.

Babbitt's policies were set aside in 2001 when Bush placed Gale Norton at the head of the Interior Department. Norton spent most of her career at the Denver-based Mountain States Legal Foundation, a conservative think tank that opposes the government's role in environmental protection. Under Norton's direction, the Department of Interior took the opposite approach of Babbitt's, weakening wilderness protections and opening formerly protected areas to gas and oil development, mining, logging, and other uses.

Those shifts in policy reveal fundamentally opposing views of the environment. While some want to preserve America's wildlands in their natural state for perpetuity, others want to use the natural resources abundant in the wilderness. This conflict is reflected in the arguments put forth in the following pages. Throughout *At Issue: How Should America's Wilderness Be Managed?* authors present differing views on the stewardship of America's wildest places.

1

America's Wilderness Must Be Carefully Managed

John C. Hendee and Chad P. Dawson

John C. Hendee is a professor and director of the University of Idaho Wilderness Research Center and editor in chief of the International Journal of Wilderness. *Chad P. Dawson is a professor at the College of Environmental Science and Forestry, State University of New York (SUNY) and co–managing editor of the* International Journal of Wilderness.

Wilderness areas in the United States face a variety of threats. As the population continues to grow, increases in air and vehicle traffic, pollution, urban sprawl, and even inconsiderate cell phone users have had a negative impact on those trying to enjoy the wilderness experience. Federal money to protect the wilderness has fallen short by hundreds of millions of dollars even as the numbers of visitors to wilderness areas increase every year. While some of the threats are irreversible, an increased concern for wilderness stewardship may reverse some of these distressing trends.

Wilderness resources and values are becoming scarcer every year as they are lost to urban sprawl roads, resource extraction, human development and intrusions from inholding landowners, global influences, and more; and even well-meaning stewardship may dilute or impact wilderness. In the future wilderness may represent the only remnants of many ecosystems, wild conditions, and opportunities in which to experience solitude and natural landscapes. The degree to which those qualities remain in wilderness tomorrow will reflect our stewardship efforts to deal with the threats to wilderness reviewed here, and more.

We define threats to wilderness here as a general concept, focusing on change agents or processes that negatively or adversely impact wilderness resource conditions and values. . . . We are talking about change agents that come directly or indirectly from human influences and not natural disturbances (e.g., lightning-caused fires, volcanoes, hurricanes, etc.). For example, increasing visitor use of wilderness areas (i.e., a change agent) can impact wilderness experiences through resulting crowding, visitor conflicts, loss of solitude, and from direct impacts on wilderness resources such as loss of vegetative ground cover at campsites, and soil erosion on trails.

We identify 17 categories of threats to wilderness and their impacts, drawing upon relevant literature and our experience and discussions with wilderness users, managers, and researchers. Some threats represent inevitable, though lamentable, global or local change, but for other threats wilderness stewardship can often make a difference. When it can, we urge wilderness managers to exercise the strongest possible protective or mitigating action.

1. *Fragmentation and isolation of wilderness as ecological islands* disconnect them from surrounding natural habitat so they may not be wholly functioning ecosystems. The 600-plus units of the National Wilderness Preservation System (NWPS) tend toward smaller units (42% are from 10,000 to 50,000 acres) rather than larger units (four wildernesses in Alaska include more than 5 million acres). The lack of large or "corridor connected" wilderness units most pronounced in the eastern United States often creates ecological "islands" more vulnerable to external and adjacent forces than areas of a million acres or more. Beyond limiting the seasonal migrations of wilderness fauna, small units may limit the mixing of flora and fauna species populations, so essential to genetic diversity and upon which their long-term health and survival depends. Some wilderness species require large undisturbed home ranges, such as wolves and grizzly bears. How to combat fragmentation and isolation of wilderness? We need comprehensive wildland management that maintains wild corridors between small wilderness areas and a wilderness designation strategy that expands and connects areas.

2. *The loss of threatened and endangered species*, and sometimes intrusive actions to save them, can threaten wilderness naturalness and solitude. While the protection of threatened or endangered species may require special efforts, including mechanical intrusions into or manipulation of the wilderness environment to favor them, such well-intentioned and legal activities may cause other impacts. We must ask how much is enough, and try to stick with the minimum, necessary tools. For example, are efforts to protect bighorn sheep in the Cabeza Prieta and other wilderness areas by providing water structures and hauling water actually necessary? Are they a justifiable intrusion on other wilderness resources and values? Are they trying to support unnaturally high sheep populations?

3. *Increasing commercial and public recreation visits* cause impacts forcing managers to increasingly regulate and control use. Recreation use and visitor management are already intense in some high-use locations, in the more popular wilderness areas, and in some places, times and seasons—even in large and remote areas. So the impacts of both commercial and recreation use and efforts to control them may threaten wilderness resources and values. Clearly, preserving wilderness naturalness and solitude requires visitor regulation in many places, though admittedly such regulation takes away the freedom and spontaneity that characterize wilderness experiences. It is a continuing balancing act, weighing the need to regulate use to control impacts against the impacts of visitor management on freedom and spontaneity of user experiences and the loss of wilderness opportunities for those turned away or limited.

4. *Livestock grazing* by domestic cattle and sheep and recreational pack

stock is legally allowed in wilderness where it existed prior to Wilderness designation, but it is often a threat to naturalness and impacts user experiences. Permitting grazing in wilderness was a compromise that was politically necessary to achieve passage of The Wilderness Act (TWA), but it impacts soil and water, and the consumption and trampling of vegetation may directly impact competing wildlife or change the composition of the forage base, which may further impact wildlife. The presence of domestic livestock also encourages predator control and may discourage programs for the recovery of endangered predators such as wolf and grizzly bear. We must respect the legality of grazing in wilderness, but we need tighter regulation of grazing in wilderness to limit its impacts.

5. *Exotic and nonnative species* are increasingly invading wilderness ecosystems, impacting naturalness, triggering ecosystem changes, and displacing native species. For example, noxious weeds such as knap-weed, star thistle, cheat grass, leafy spurge, and others have outcompeted native species and are rapidly spreading in wilderness. Control efforts are not benign either, as secondary impacts may result from biological, chemical, or physical control mechanisms, and they may not work. The invasion of wilderness by nonnative species, especially noxious weeds, is a very serious threat to wilderness naturalness. What to do? This is a complex dilemma for wilderness managers, with no easy answers that work. But when considering control options, first do no harm.

Preserving wilderness naturalness and solitude requires visitor regulation in many places, though admittedly such regulation takes away the freedom and spontaneity that characterize wilderness experiences.

---

6. *Excessive administrative access, facilities, and intrusive management* can threaten naturalness and wilderness values. Mechanized access to wilderness by managers is legal under TWA when it is the minimum method to accomplish a legitimate and necessary wilderness or endangered species purpose, including facility construction and maintenance. Such management may be in support of any legitimate wilderness purpose, such as visitor management, grazing, mining, commercial outfitting, maintaining historic structures, or trail construction. Recent wilderness designation laws, like the California Desert Protection Act of 1994, expanded management access by providing for mechanized intrusions to support fish and wildlife management (not just endangered species) and law enforcement in the 69 BLM [Bureau of Land Management] wilderness areas it established. With mechanized access to wilderness so easily justified, management restraint and judgment is especially important in not abusing the privilege. We still need to ask: is mechanized access really necessary? Is it the minimum tool that will work?

7. *Adjacent land management and use can impact wilderness* and is a concern for managers because they often have little or no control over what happens beyond the wilderness boundary. A survey of U.S. wilderness managers in 1995 reported 60 different perceived impacts that adjacent land uses had on the wilderness; the top five were: fire management, mil-

itary overflights, exotic plant introduction, air pollution, and off-road vehicle use. Wilderness managers need to expand their awareness, communication, and educational efforts beyond wilderness boundaries and seek better coordination of adjacent land management activities to minimize their impacts on wilderness.

Past fire suppression allowed tremendous fuel loads to build up, contributing to today's larger and more intense wildfires.

---

8. *Inholdings of private or public lands* within wilderness areas can create impacts because inholders have a right to reasonable access and use of their lands. Some inholdings contain historic impacts, such as old mining claims or homesteads, others serve as active ranches or private retreats, giving their owners prime access to wilderness surroundings. Sometimes motorized access is granted to inholders on primitive roads, by aircraft, or by boats. Inholdings may be used by commercial outfitters and provide sites for supporting facilities and services (e.g., stock facilities, aircraft landing fields), access (e.g., interior private roads), and visitor facilities (e.g., outfitter camps, private dwellings). Wilderness managers need courage here to stand as firm as possible against nonconforming activities taking place on inholdings. A current example is a proposal by an inholder in California's and Palen McCoy Wilderness to build an access road to haul a large telescope and well-drilling equipment, all to support private retreats to the site. . . .

9. *Mining and extraction from established claims* is allowed in wilderness, although further mineral exploration has been phased out under TWA. For example, oil development is being considered in Alaska and silver mining on existing claims near the Cabinet Mountains Wilderness in Montana. The negative impacts of mining to wilderness naturalness and wildness are extensive. Even old mines that have been "played out" may continue to impact wilderness with their residual buildings, junk heaps, mine tailings, and roads that continue to erode and which invite vehicle trespass, not to mention the visual and ecological impacts of these historical remnants. Managers need public support for imposing conditions as strict as possible on current mining operations, and public participation in efforts to clean up the messes left at old mining sites, such as public lands day cleanup projects and other volunteer rehabilitation efforts.

10. *Wild land fire suppression*, adjacent to and inside wilderness, is changing ecosystems by reducing natural fire frequencies, leading to changes in ecosystem structure and composition. Allowing natural processes like fire to continue to function in their natural role in wilderness ecosystems and landscapes is now recognized as important to providing diversity and natural variation. But the tendency is for federal agencies to suppress most fires, in part because of the fear and risk that they would spread to adjacent, non-wilderness lands and, in part, because of political pressure to suppress them. The massive stand-replacing fires that have occurred in recent years (in 2000 more than 6 million acres burned in 80,000 wildland fires) are confirming that past fire suppression

allowed tremendous fuel loads to build up, contributing to today's larger and more intense wildfires. Wilderness has not been immune from this fuel buildup. Difficult as it is and will be, restoring natural fire regimes in wilderness is important to the integrity of wilderness ecosystems.

11. *Polluted air* is a threat to wilderness naturalness because of its physical and biological impacts and the accompanying reduced visibility that may impact wilderness experiences. [Studies] have reported that visual impairment from pollution can cause visitors to change trip schedules or to choose another location that has better visibility. In the eastern United States acid rain from industrial and urban emissions can be especially harmful to high-elevation ecosystems. In the West, in 1996 the U.S. Forest Service (USFS) notified the state of Washington that visibility in the Alpine Lakes and Goat Rocks Wilderness areas was adversely impacted by a coal-fueled power plant in Centralia, Washington, and subsequently a mediated settlement for air quality improvement was completed. The air quality in wilderness serves as an important indicator of overall ambient air quality, and this connects wilderness to concerns of the larger society. Wilderness's role in monitoring air quality for the nation provides an excellent opportunity to explain how wilderness serves everyone, even those who will never go there.

12. *Water storage facilities require the legal reconstruction and maintenance of dams and reservoirs in wilderness for water storage*, thereby impacting wilderness solitude and naturalness. Such storage is important because of historic use of wilderness water for irrigation in valleys below, and growing competition in the western United States for water to maintain "in stream" flows for fisheries, aquatic biota [flora and fauna], and wildlife. But maintenance and reconstruction of water storage facilities in wilderness are very controversial because of the mechanized intrusions that are required. Again, the mandate is for wilderness naturalness. Water is an increasingly scarce commodity, the best of which may come from wilderness. How can we do what's needed and required while minimizing impacts?

"The resources committed to protect and manage wilderness have not kept pace with our needs."

---

13. *Advanced technology* threatens to reduce wilderness solitude with electronic communication, navigation devices, and mechanical transport equipment that dilute remoteness, risk, and discovery. Technology also intrudes with high-tech outerwear and backpacking gear that insulate visitors from historic wilderness experiences. The use of GPS equipment, cell phones, radios, and other electronic technology by search-and-rescue personnel is generally accepted, much like the use of high-technology ropes and climbing gear. The use of mechanical transport in search-and-rescue operations is also accepted when human life is at stake. But the availability of modern electronic communication, navigation devices, and mechanized access may give visitors a false sense of security and contribute to irresponsible behaviors based on their assumption that rescue is only a cellphone call and helicopter flight away. But why can't users be asked to observe more of a minimum-tool approach to wilderness recreation? We think their

wilderness experiences and benefits would be better for it, and we urge wilderness managers to provide leadership in transmitting this message.

14. *Motorized and mechanical equipment trespass and legal use* can dilute wilderness solitude and damage resources. For example, operators of snow-mobiles and all terrain vehicles (ATVs) can travel cross-country and enter a wilderness area inadvertently, or the trespass may be deliberate for convenience or recreational purposes, and go undiscovered in remote locations. Management's use of motorized vehicles and mechanical equipment is legal in wilderness where it is the minimum method for accomplishing a legitimate wilderness purpose, and in some areas for such activities as wildlife management and law enforcement. Examples that might be approved are helicopters for special projects, ATVs for beach patrols, four-wheel-drive vehicles for wildlife management activities, and chain saws for trail construction. When wilderness visitors see managers using mechanized vehicles or equipment, it affects how they view them and shapes visitors' views of what wilderness should be. To the contrary, when visitors see wilderness managers—and researchers—carrying out their work with primitive tools, it sends a positive message of respect for the wilderness and conveys that living with primitive skills and tools is possible!

15. *Aircraft noise from aircraft overflights* of wilderness by commercial and military aircraft cause noise and visual pollution, and dilute solitude with a dramatic reminder of modern society to which wilderness users object. There are also legal private and public airfields in wilderness in Montana and Idaho used by private visitors as well as outfitters moving supplies and customers. In Alaska the preexisting use of aircraft, especially floatplanes, continues in designated wilderness. Lowlevel military overflights can be traumatic to wilderness visitors and resident fauna, though such privilege is legally sanctioned in many areas. As overflights and the use of aircraft to access wilderness grows, wilderness managers must determine what management discretion is available to limit them or mitigate their impacts, and then face objections from the military, private pilot, and wilderness outfitter organizations that do not want such privileges limited. We hope wilderness managers will exercise their fullest possible discretion and influence to keep overflights and air access into wilderness from escalating, and reducing them when possible.

16. *Urbanization and encroaching urban development* toward wilderness boundaries dilutes wilderness with civilized sights, sounds, and diminished remoteness. Urban sprawl has dramatically affected wilderness conditions with smog, encroaching roads that make access easier, noise, and casual day use in urban-proximate wildernesses such as San Gorgonio outside Los Angeles. We fear that increasingly diverse and urbanized visitors to wilderness may be satisfied with trips to crowded and heavily impacted wilderness due to their lack of previous experience in more pristine areas and may develop a wilderness frame of reference more tolerant of crowding and oblivious to impacts. Yet these users may need the respite offered by wilderness the most. We urge managers to expand their educational efforts about what wilderness is, what it is meant to provide, why management is necessary—and to do everything possible to see that diverse, urban visitors have the chance to enjoy a wilderness experience. We need the support and understanding of these people to sustain wilderness.

17. *Lack of political, and thus financial support for wilderness protection*

and management is a great concern of the federal agencies, as expressed by then chief of the USFS Mike Dombeck, ". . . the resources committed to protect and manage wilderness have not kept pace with our needs, . . . particularly for field work budgets and staff" (1999). The evidence of such neglect is wide and deep. Long overdue wilderness plans are still in progress or have not been started. Others are in need of revision and updating. Numerous roadless and wilderness study areas are being evaluated to determine if they should be added to the NWPS, and many areas recommended for wilderness years ago have not been acted upon by Congress. This lack of political and financial support for wilderness stewardship may be one of the most serious threats to wilderness in the long run. Funding for people and programs is required to maintain high standards of wilderness naturalness and solitude. We all need to help meet this threat by speaking out for wilderness to elected officials, and enlisting help from organizations and the larger public to whom elected officials are responsive.

A stronger stand

This list of 17 threats to wilderness oversimplifies them, their seriousness, their current escalation, and how they might be addressed. We encourage a stronger stand against them by managers, and proactive support for manager resistance to them by the wilderness community. Reducing the dilution of wilderness resources and values by these threats and impacts is essential to help wilderness achieve its potential.

2

The Free Market Can Protect Wilderness More Effectively than Government

Michael De Alessi

Michael De Alessi is director of the Center for Private Conservation, a project of the Competitive Enterprise Institute in Washington, D.C.

Government agencies have not succeeded in protecting wilderness. Raging wildfires are ravaging federal lands while other areas are threatened by overgrazing, illegal hunting, and other problems. Meanwhile, those who own wilderness on private property have been successful where the U.S. Forest Service has failed. Private ownership has been a positive factor for some who have preserved and improved wild lands and helped threatened species recover. Some are motivated by esthetic considerations while others preserve wilderness areas to make money on camping, hiking, and other recreational activities. Whatever the aims of the landowners, private ownership has been a positive force in wilderness management in some areas.

D espite much ecological pessimism in recent years, the gains in environmental quality around the world in the last few decades have been astounding. People are living longer, the air is getting cleaner, and agriculture is becoming more productive, freeing up more land for wildlife and forest growth.

Yet, strangely enough, the general view of the environment's future seems to be a dim one, and the issues of environmental protection and conservation seem to be growing in importance all the time.

Why the disparity? One reason is that although entrepreneurs have largely driven the gains in agriculture and technology that have improved environmental quality, they are still not viewed as trustworthy stewards of the environment—despite the generally dismal track record of governmental conservation programs. Widespread fisheries depletion, overgrazed and overcrowded national parks, the forest fires that ravaged the Southwest in 2000, and the failure to recover endangered species are all potent reasons to search for more viable alternatives.

Private conservation is one such alternative. It provides environmental benefits through the institutions of private ownership and the marketplace, which create incentives to protect and enhance natural resources. And whether they are profit seekers or simply motivated by a love of nature, private conservationists tap into the entrepreneurial spirit, providing a variety of approaches to solving environmental problems.

Even some traditional environmentalists recognize private conservation's potential. For example, Brent Blackwelder, president of the "green" organization Friends of the Earth, has said, "While I don't believe that private efforts alone are the answer, recognizing the ingenuity, commitment, and effectiveness of private stewards is imperative."

In the United States, private conservation predates the nation's independence. When [Thomas] Jefferson saw the Natural Bridge of Virginia, a remarkable natural limestone formation, it so inspired him that he bought it from King George of England in 1774. It is still privately owned today and open to the public, yet its natural setting remains unspoiled.

Saving wood ducks and the woods

Another early private-conservation success story was the recovery of the wood duck in the United States. Due to hunting and government incentives to fill in wetland habitat toward the end of the nineteenth century, the wood duck population was dwindling. But conservationists found that it was easy to create artificial nesting habitat for this species, and soon duck boxes were being placed around the country. Everyone from Boy Scouts to wildlife biologists helped put up the boxes, often on private land. Today, the wood duck is one of the commonest waterfowl species in the United States.

Unfortunately, helping rare and endangered species has gone from being an attractive proposition to a liability. Under the U.S. Endangered Species Act (ESA), having a rare or endangered species can mean a loss of rights to private land. The size and scope of such measures as the ESA have discouraged many private conservation efforts and have overshadowed past successes such as the recovery of the wood duck.

> *"While I don't believe that private efforts alone are the answer, recognizing the ingenuity, commitment, and effectiveness of private stewards is imperative."*

In fact, some of the best examples of private conservation arose in direct opposition to government programs of their day. Hawk Mountain in Pennsylvania has been a privately owned sanctuary since it was purchased in 1934 by the early suffragette [women's voting rights advocate] Rosalie Edge. Before 1934, vast numbers of raptors [birds of prey] would glide by Hawk Mountain on their southbound autumn migrations, where an army of hunters would fell them and collect the government bounty on raptors.

Early conservationists lobbied to stop the slaughter, but their pleas fell on deaf ears. So Edge simply raised some money and bought the mountaintop in 1934, hiring a warden to patrol and protect both the property and the birds. Today, it is one of the premier hawk-watching sites in the world, visited by 80,000 people annually.

Because Audubon owns the land, it was able to weigh the benefits of drilling against the environmental hazards—and to take whatever precautions it thought necessary to protect the birds.

Forests offer another stark contrast between public and private management. The national-forest system was set up initially for logging, but over the past 30 years that focus has changed to preserving wilderness—that is, doing nothing with the land. The worst part of this has been the government's fire-suppression policy. Instead of large, beautiful forests with big trees and green, open areas underneath, the policy has created a dense underbrush, so that now, when there is a fire, it burns hot enough to reach the crowns of the bigger trees, killing them, whereas before this was not the case. The trees are also more susceptible to disease and pests such as bark beetles.

On private lands, however, there has tended to be salvage harvest of trees, work to limit noxious pests, and control of the undergrowth. Many private forest owners are also moving away from logging as their sole revenue source toward such fee-based activities as camping, hiking, and hunting. In fact, due to current management practices on public lands, George Reiger, the conservation editor at *Field and Stream* magazine, believes that "the future of hunting for millions of American sportsmen will be on privately managed farms, forests, and rangelands.". . .

From halibut to salmon

Ownership rights are also radically changing the way entrepreneurs look at fisheries. When regulatory controls are the norm (as they are in most of the world's fisheries), fishermen look for innovative ways to beat the system. An extreme example was the Alaska halibut and sablefish fishery, where regulators tried to reduce harvests by shortening the fishing season. Before long, what was once a nearly six-month season had been reduced to 48 hours—with no reduction in the catch! People simply figured out how to catch more fish in less time.

Today, that fishery is one of the best managed in the United States. An individual transferable quota (ITQ) system allots a certain percentage of the total catch to each fisherman. Now there's no more race to fish and no more huge investments in the capacity necessary to catch a year's worth of fish in two days. A recent letter to the *Alaska Fisherman's Journal* summed up reaction to the change: "We fish better weather, deliver a better product, and have a better market. This is a better deal."

The key to innovation and environmental stewardship may be more than markets, however. Another crucial factor is private ownership—which Alaska fishermen do not have. They own neither the fish nor the fishery but just the right to harvest fish, and the government can take this away at any time. As a result, the fishing business is improved, but little has changed about managing the fishery.

A real private-conservation alternative exists under English common law. In Britain, for example, there are private, heritable rights to fish for salmon in rivers and streams. The owners of these rights have a recourse against polluters, because the latter are damaging the fishermen's rights as surely as if they were throwing rocks through someone's window.

Even in Washington State, where there is no such right to clean water, the fact that oyster beds can be privately owned has led to cleaner water. Oysters are filter feeders, which depend on clean water, and so the oyster growers have been the most vigilant protectors of water quality in that state. According to Dick Wilson, a Washington oyster grower, "Willapa is the cleanest bay in the country, and it is the oystermen who have kept it that way.". . .

An environmental group's oil wells

Another example of how private ownership leads to trade-offs rather than conflicts is a private sanctuary in Louisiana owned by the Louisiana Audubon Society. National Audubon has vehemently opposed drilling for oil on public lands in any number of cases, yet there are actually some wells in the Rainey Wildlife Sanctuary. Rainey is such an important bird sanctuary that the public is not allowed to visit. But because Audubon owns the land, it was able to weigh the benefits of drilling against the environmental hazards—and to take whatever precautions it thought necessary to protect the birds.

Of course, many companies and individuals aren't good stewards of the environment—but once again, it seems to be a question of ownership. Degraded resources, whether rivers, forests, or airsheds, are generally unowned. Timber leases in the United States are one example. Timber companies tend to behave very differently depending on whether they harvest trees from their own property or from public lands. Private timberland owners tend not only to invest in the forest's future health but to consider fee-based alternatives to logging such as hunting or hiking, which they cannot do with a short-term lease on public forest lands.

Legal restrictions on how rights may be exercised can impede private conservation. Until recently, water rights in Oregon were based on a "use it or lose it" regime, in which leaving water instream for salmon was not considered a use. This created conflict between farmers and the environmental community. Once the law was changed to include instream flows in the definition of "use," however, an entrepreneurial conservation group called the Oregon Water Trust became very successful at buying water rights to leave the water instream.

What Thomas Jefferson understood so well in the eighteenth century—that private ownership is the surest way to protect something—has become less influential in recent years. But the concept has hardly gone away. Human ingenuity and the entrepreneurial spirit underlie just about every private-conservation success story. When private property institutions prevail, problem solvers become remarkably resourceful at protecting and enhancing the value of what they own—for reasons as different as profit and aesthetics—whether it be fisheries and forests or backyard gardens.

3

Roads Through the Wilderness Cause Irreparable Harm

Ayesha Ercelawn

Ayesha Ercelawn is an author who has published many articles about the environment as well as a children's book about New Zealand.

While the wilderness is managed for many activities, few uses impact plants and animals more severely than logging and the roads built to service timber-cutting sites. Logging destroys wilderness habitat that is home to dozens of threatened and endangered species. Roads segment the forests, creating dangerous conditions for creatures attempting to cross. Clear-cut areas and service roads promote landslides and erosion that is detrimental to streams and lakes. Such disturbances of the wilderness also allow non-native species to establish themselves, usually to the detriment of native plants and animals. Logging also promotes disease and insect infestations that harm remaining wild areas.

Roads displace species sensitive to disturbance or dependent on forest interior habitat. For example, species like grizzly bears, wolves, and elk avoid otherwise suitable habitat near roads. They may modify their home range, and they have been shown to select areas with lower road densities than the average on the landscape. As a result, high-quality habitat becomes effectively unavailable to them.

Roads also create barriers to the movement of many species. In particular, small animals such as salamanders, frogs, and mice will rarely cross roads or are killed by vehicles when crossing. As barriers to dispersal, roads isolate populations on one side of the road from those on the other. Biologists fear a likely consequence of this isolation . . . is, over the long-term, increased vulnerability of some species to inbreeding or environmental catastrophes. Larger species such as moose, white-tailed deer, and mule deer also have high rates of mortality due to roadkill. The impact of high roadkill rates on species' total population number is not

Ayesha Ercelawn, "End of the Road: The Adverse Ecological Impacts of Roads and Logging: A Compilation of Independently Reviewed Research," www.nrdc.org. Copyright © by Natural Resources Defense Council, Inc. Reproduced by permission.

thoroughly understood, but roads may act as ecological "sinks" (areas of net loss) for some species, endangering their continuing viability.

Species that live in the forest interior are also adversely affected by logging, which fragments habitat by destroying old-growth and mature forest and by creating poor quality habitat "edges" in otherwise continuous forest. Species that prefer old-growth and closed canopy forest, such as martens, California red-backed voles, northern flying squirrels, and red-backed salmanders, to mention a few, have declined in abundance in logged forests relative to unlogged forests. These species' decline in turn has impacts on other parts of the ecosystem. For instance, a reduction in salamander populations (which are an integral part of the forest food chain) affects bird and mammal species that rely on them as food, as well as forest floor ecology and nutrient cycles.

Research has also shown that forest interior birds are sensitive to disturbance, whether in the form of roads, logging, or the increased access they provide to nest predators or parasitic cowbirds. Breeding success has declined in many of these affected areas. For example, bald eagle nesting success is lower near clearcuts. In eastern forests, cowbirds have invaded the edges (and in some cases, the interior) of many forest fragments. This species parasitizes the nests of other bird species, destroying their eggs or young and laying its own eggs in the nest instead. Research has shown that this behavior may be partly responsible for the population declines of many . . . migrant bird species.

[Examples of] displacement of wildlife:
- Grizzly bear use of suitable habitat in Montana declined as road density and road traffic increased. . . .
- Wolves in Alaska avoided roads that were open to regular public use. . . .
- Mountain lions avoided improved dirt roads and hard-surfaced roads and selected home range areas with lower densities of these road types.
- Female Roosevelt elk reduced their daily movements, core area size, and home range size, and therefore, their energy needs, when disturbance due to vehicular access on roads was limited by gate closures. . . .
- Roads impeded movement by amphibians and could result in population isolation. Despite some speculation, road ruts and ditches have not been shown to provide successful amphibian breeding habitat rather than acting as ecological traps. Amphibians play a key role in the forest ecosystem, affecting nutrient cycling and also serving as high quality prey for many species. . . .

[Examples of] loss of habitat:
- Mountain lions avoided logging areas and established home ranges in areas with lower road densities than the average in the area. . . .
- Red-backed salamanders, sensitive to forest moisture and temperature levels, were more abundant in old-growth forest and 60-year-old second-growth than in clearcuts or selective logged forest. Salamanders are a critical part of the forest food chain: they are important food sources for birds and mammals, and as predators themselves, they cycle large amounts of energy through the forest ecosystem. . . .

[Examples of] reduced nesting success:
- The density of bald eagle nests in southeast Alaska decreased with proximity to clearcuts. . . .
- Three of four forest interior bird species declined in abundance after logging, whether clearcutting or lower intensity logging. . . .

Spread of tree diseases and bark beetles

Logging and road construction have increased the incidence of damaging or lethal tree diseases, including annosus root disease, Armillaria, laminated root rot, black-stain root disease, and Indian paint fungus. Tree stumps have a high likelihood of infection, become centers of infection in a stand, and facilitate the spread of a disease to adjacent, living trees. For some diseases, such as black-stain root disease, woody debris left after thinning attracts insects that are vectors for infection. For at least one disease, Port-orford-cedar root rot, road construction and logging equipment have been directly linked to the spread of the disease to new stands. Black-stain root disease has also been found to occur at higher rates along roads and skid trails.

Trees stressed by disease are more susceptible to attack by bark beetles. For example, ponderosa pines infected with black-stain root disease have suffered higher bark beetle attack rates than undiseased trees. Attempts to mitigate some of these problems have not been easy or fully successfully. Stump treatments, such as borax, are not one hundred percent effective, while other efforts, such as stump removal, damage essential ecosystem functions through soil compaction. . . .

Promotion of insect infestations

Forest edges created by logging or road construction sustain higher populations of tree pest species such as the tent caterpillar, jack pine budworm, and gypsy moth. Possible mechanisms for this include increased larval development due to higher light levels and increased mortality of natural pathogens.

Biologists predict that logging and habitat destruction will increase the severity of a variety of insect outbreaks because the loss of habitat diversity and old-growth forest has meant a decrease in the diversity of natural pest predators. Natural predators of the western spruce budworm for instance include ant and bird species whose habitat needs include large standing and downed logs that are reduced or eliminated by logging.

[Examples of] insect infestations:
- Forest fragmentation due to cleared forest increased the duration of tent caterpillar outbreaks. . . .
- Abrupt edges along mature jack pine stands increased the levels of defoliation by jack pine budworm in Michigan.
- Trees at forest edges created by roads had 2.4 times more gypsy moth egg masses than trees in the forest interior.

[Examples of] loss of ecological complexity:
- A diversity of predators is important for preventing pest outbreaks.
- Old-growth and roadless areas, with their greater diversity of composition, structure, and predators, are predicted to be less vulnerable

to pest outbreaks than forests simplified through management. . . .
• Ants, important predators of the western spruce budworm, require sufficient down wood in a range of sizes and decomposition stages.

Invasion by harmful non-native plant and animal species

Roads facilitate the spread of invasive non-native (exotic) plants, animals, and insects. For example, vehicles can transport the seeds of exotic plants to new areas. Reduced canopy cover (with correspondingly higher light levels) and increased soil disturbance along roads have favored numerous exotic plant species, including Oriental bittersweet and spotted knapweed, as well as exotic ant species such as the red imported fire ant and the Argentine ant. Over time, some exotic species spread from roadsides into adjacent, undisturbed areas.

> *Forest interior birds are sensitive to disturbance, whether in the form of roads, logging, or the increased access they provide to nest predators.*

Exotic species disrupt natural ecosystem processes and the species that depend on them. For example, exotic plants have been shown to replace native understory vegetation, inhibit seedling regeneration, and change soil nutrient cycling. Some weedy species can cause higher erosion rates or change fire regimes. The abundance and diversity of native ants has decreased in areas invaded by the red imported fire ant or the Argentine ant. This can change the entire food base for other species. The decline in other species, such as the northern bobwhite, has been directly documented in habitat infested with exotic ants.

[Examples of] invasion by non-native species:
• Non-native plant species occurred on high-use, low-use, and abandoned forest roads, with the greatest frequency on roads with the highest level of disturbance and lowest percentage of canopy cover.
• Exotic annual plants invaded an ecological reserve in California along a pipeline corridor and were still dominant in the corridor 10 years after the disturbance occurred.
• Oriental bittersweet, an exotic vine of the eastern United States, responded vigorously to increased light intensity after disturbances such as road construction, [or] logging. . . .

Damage to soil resources and tree growth

Logging and road construction compact soils, disturb or destroy organic layers, and cause high rates of soil erosion. Soil compaction, which can last for several decades, is typically measured by changes in soil . . . density. . . . Trees' access to nutrients and water is reduced because of restricted root growth in compacted soils, reduced water infiltration rates, and decreased oxygen and water available to root systems. Soil compaction also has a detrimental impact on microorganism communities, which play a critical role in nutrient cycling and tree growth. The loss of organic layers also affects mycorrhizal fungi, which are important to many tree species in accessing nutrients. As a result of this damage to soil resources, trees can suffer from moisture stress, reduced growth rates, inability to establish seedlings, and reduced resilience in the long term.

Compacted soils are also more susceptible to surface erosion. The frequency of mass erosion events, such as debris slides, also increases in landscapes that have been roaded or logged, thus increasing total soil loss. . . .

This loss of soil due to erosion not only reduces the productivity of the local site by removing top, nutrient-rich layers of soil, but the sediment that is generated often runs into streams, where it has a range of detrimental impacts on aquatic ecosystems. . . .

Impacts on aquatic ecosystems

Roads and logging can significantly degrade stream ecoystems by introducing high volumes of sediment into streams, changing natural streamflow patterns, and altering [the] stream channel. . . . The frequency of landslides in steep terrain is higher in roaded areas and in forests that have been clearcut. Much of the resultant eroded soil ends up in streams. Fine sediment from road surfaces runs into streams during storm events. . . .

Streamflow patterns can change in watersheds that are roaded and/or have been logged. Roads, ditches, and new gullies form new, large networks of flow paths across the landscape; this changes the rate at which water reaches streams. As a result, peak discharge volumes in some watersheds are higher and after large storms begin earlier than they would in undisturbed watersheds.

The frequency of mass erosion events, such as debris slides, also increases in landscapes that have been roaded or logged.

These changes in stream habitat affect the health of aquatic organisms. The survival rates of many salmonid [juvenile salmon] species, for instance, decrease as fine sediment levels increase. Deposition of fine sediment on the stream bed degrades spawning areas, reduces pool refuge habitat, decreases winter refuge areas for juveniles, and impedes feeding visibility. For example, survival rates of coho salmon, chum salmon, and steelhead trout fry decrease as stream sediment levels increase. Sensitive amphibian and invertebrate [insect and mollusk] species are also adversely affected by increased sediment loads, decreasing in abundance and/or diversity. Thus, large-sized aquatic invertebrate species may be replaced by smaller-sized species. Changes to aquatic invertebrate communities not only affect the food supply available to other stream organisms such as fish, but also to non-aquatic forest species. As adults, stream invertebrates emerge from streams and occupy . . . forests, where they are an important source of food for birds, bats, and various other mammals.

Changes in stream channel structure lead to decreases in the habitat available to fish and other organisms. In addition, increases in stream peak discharge volumes and/or sediment loads can affect egg survival rates of

salmon adapted to natural stream flows or streambed scour rates. . . .
[Examples of] increases in-sediment and altered streamflows: . . .

- Roads were responsible for 61% of the soil volume displaced by erosion in northwestern California.
- Clearcutting increased the frequency of mass soil movements from hillsides. . . .
- The volume of fine sediment present in streams increased in direct proportion to logging in the watershed and stream crossings by roads.
- Almost 30 years after clearcut logging occurred, average and peak stream flows in the watershed studied were still higher than pre-logging flows. . . .

[Examples of] adverse impacts on aquatic species:

- Coho and chum salmon fry survival declined after logging and associated increases in fine sediment deposited in spawning areas.
- Salmonids avoided water with suspended sediment in Alaskan streams and lakes.
- Basins with more than 25% of their area logged had lower stream habitat diversity, as measured by the number of pools and pieces of wood, than basins with less than 25% of their area logged.

4

Roadless Rules
Threaten the Wilderness

Randal O'Toole

Randal O'Toole is a forest economist in Oregon and founder of the Thoreau Institute, a conservative organization that brings together environmentalists, timber company representatives, ranchers, miners, and government officials to find solutions to environmental problems.

In 1999 President Clinton proposed a rule to prohibit road building on millions of acres of federal land. Although Clinton failed to justify this massive undertaking with scientific evidence, in 2003, after several court battles, the roadless rule went into effect. A comprehensive ban on road building that includes wilderness areas such as deserts, forests, and mountain meadows makes no sense from a land-management perspective, as each area has its own unique environmental qualities. Many of the areas where roads are prohibited are prone to catastrophic wildfires. Without roads, fires in these areas are nearly impossible to extinguish. In light of this fact, the decision whether to build roads in wild areas should be left to local forest managers, not bureaucrats in Washington, D.C. Road building should only be prohibited after thorough scientific analysis has determined the move is in the best interest of the forest ecosystem.

Editor's Note: The proposed rules discussed in the following selection went into effect in 2003.

In October 1999, President Clinton directed the Forest Service to "provide appropriate long-term protection" for inventoried roadless areas in the national forests. Clinton added that the agency should "determine whether such protection is warranted for any smaller 'roadless' areas not yet inventoried," an unknown number of areas smaller than 5,000 acres.

The Forest Service has responded to Clinton's order by publishing a three-and-one-half page draft roadless area rule accompanied by a 700-page draft environmental impact statement (DEIS). The Forest Service's proposed action is to ban all roads in the 43 million acres of inventoried roadless areas outside of the Tongass National Forest while deferring decisions about the Tongass and uninventoried roadless areas to local Forest Service managers.

The stated purpose of the proposed rulemaking is to protect water quality, biological diversity, wildlife habitat, forest health, dispersed recreation opportunities, and other public benefits, as well as to save money on road construction. . . .

Despite the impressive length of the DEIS, the Forest Service has failed to justify its proposal in three major ways. First, it has failed to show why a blanket, nationwide rule is needed to protect important values in roadless areas. In some cases, the economic and environmental benefits of such a rule are likely to be less than the economic and environmental costs of not being able to build a road.

Second, it has failed to provide any data indicating that all 51 million acres of roadless lands require the proposed levels of protection. Indeed, some of the few quantitative data in the DEIS suggest that many roadless areas are in need of ecosystem restoration activities that will require some level of construction.

Third, the DEIS fails to consider alternatives that could comply with President Clinton's directive without the high environmental risks or economic costs associated with the proposed action. One such alternative would be to prohibit permanent roads but allow low-impact temporary roads needed for forest health or ecosystem restoration. Such roads could be closed when no longer needed, thus minimizing economic and environmental costs.

Decades of controversial debates

The Forest Service's draft environmental impact statement (DEIS) for roadless area conservation is the most recent step in a decades-old debate about the fate of relatively undeveloped lands in the 192-million acre National Forest System. The debate began in the 1920s when a few Forest Service employees suggested that the best use of some national forest lands might be to leave them alone.

In the 1930s, a Forest Service official and wilderness advocate named Bob Marshall convinced national forest managers across the country to declare millions of acres of land as "wilderness" or "primitive" areas. But in the 1950s, surging demand for national forest timber led managers to declassify many wilderness and primitive areas so they could build roads and harvest the trees. This led wilderness proponents to convince Congress to pass the 1964 Wilderness Act, which set aside some areas and directed the Forest Service to evaluate other roadless areas for their wilderness suitability.

Spurred by environmentalists, the Forest Service went through a roadless area review and evaluation (RARE) process in the early 1970s. But the courts ruled that this national review was inadequate to comply with the National Environmental Policy Act's requirement that environmental impacts be fully disclosed. So the Forest Service rolled roadless area reviews into a land-use planning process it was undertaking on each national forest. But environmentalists were often able to persuade the Chief of the Forest Service that the local plans were poorly written and biased against roadless area protection.

In response to increasing controversies over roadless areas [in the 1970s], the Carter Administration initiated a new review process, known as RARE II. But decisions made by this process remained controversial and the courts again ruled that the national document was legally inadequate.

During the 1980s, Congress passed new wilderness legislation on a state-by-state basis. Such legislation typically specified that most roadless lands not designated as wilderness would be available, without further analysis, for roads or other developments. The legislation also typically stated that these remaining roadless areas were not to be considered for wilderness during forest planning, but could be considered in later forest plan updates.

The 1980s wilderness legislation seemed to put the roadless area debate to rest. Yet the debate simply continued on other terms, as environmentalists continued to challenge national forest roads and timber cutting on other grounds, such as that undeveloped forests were needed for habitat by threatened or endangered species. These challenges plus internal changes within the Forest Service led to a dramatic, 70-percent decline in national forest timber sales after 1990.

Long-term protection

Through most of the 1990s, the term "roadless areas" has pretty much been replaced by more sophisticated debates over wildlife habitats, watershed, and other issues. But in October 1999, President Clinton reopened the roadless area question by directing the Forest Service to "provide appropriate long-term protection for most or all of these currently inventoried 'roadless' areas, and to determine whether such protection is warranted for any smaller 'roadless' areas not yet inventoried." . . .

The inventoried roadless areas cover about 54 million acres of the 192-million acre National Forest System. About 2.8 million acres have been roaded since the inventory, so President Clinton's directive applies to the remaining 51 million acres. These 51 million acres, about 8 million of which are in the Tongass National Forest [in Alaska], range from deep, dark old-growth forests to tall grass prairie; from Rocky Mountain alpine meadows to the Great Basin [west of the Rocky Mountains]. Indeed, other than the fact that they haven't had roads built in them, these areas have little in common.

Given [the] wide geographic range and ecological diversity, it is difficult to imagine how a blanket, nationwide prescription for roadless area management can make any sense.

President Clinton's directive is widely considered to be partly due to his desire to leave a conservation "legacy." But it may also be a recognition that the Forest Service is beginning to review and revise many national forest plans written ten to fifteen years ago. Under the terms of the state wilderness laws passed during the 1980s, as part of these plans, the Forest Service would be required to once again consider any remaining roadless lands for wilderness. The proposed rule would transform the nature of such decisions since managers would no longer have the option to propose uses that require roads. . . .

Three different actions for three different types of areas

The DEIS actually contains three different proposals for three different types of roadless areas: inventoried roadless lands outside the Tongass, inventoried roadless lands in the Tongass, and roadless lands in areas that are not yet inventoried.

1. For *roadless portions of inventoried roadless areas outside of the Tongass National Forest*, an estimated 43 million acres, the DEIS proposes to ban new road construction, with limited exceptions if roads are needed to protect public health and safety or in certain other cases.

2. For *roadless portions of inventoried roadless areas in the Tongass National Forest*, an estimated 8 million acres, the DEIS proposes to defer any decision until 2004 and let that decision be made as a part of the forest planning review process. Because Tongass timber sales have fallen to very low levels, the agency expects that few new roads will be built in roadless areas before this decision is made.

3. For *unroaded areas that are not inventoried as roadless*, an unestimated amount of land, the plan proposes to allow local Forest Service managers to decide how to manage such areas in the course of forest and project planning. The proposal sets no minimum size limit on such roadless lands but leaves this to the local forest managers' discretion.

The second and third proposals are not significantly different from the current direction; at most, they direct planners to give recognition to roadless areas whose fate would be decided in forest planning anyway. The first proposal represents the biggest change in policy and is the subject of most of these comments.

To describe such areas as "natural," in the sense that they are uninfluenced by modern civilization, is factually incorrect.

The actual rule that covers all three proposals fills about three-and-one-half pages of the draft environmental impact statement. The rest of the DEIS fills more than 700 pages, including 200 pages of maps. The other 500 pages are filled mostly with qualitative and subjective prose. Indeed, though covering a subject that has been studied for decades, the document has surprisingly little quantified information.

Is a blanket proscription appropriate?

This proposal covers hundreds of different roadless areas covering tens of millions of acres located in thirty-eight states and Puerto Rico. From the cactus deserts of Arizona to the rainforests of the Olympic Peninsula, from the mixed hardwood forests of Georgia to the nearly pure Douglas-fir forests of western Oregon, roadless areas vary tremendously across the nation. Clearly, the roadless areas contain a wide range of ecological types. Wide variations can exist within just a short distance. Many people crossing the Cascade Mountain crest will note an abrupt change from the Douglas-fir-western hemlock forests on the west side to the ponderosa pine–true fir forests on the east side. Cove hardwoods of the south differ from the upland hardwoods. Scrawny lodgepole pine forests in the interior West may grow just a few miles away from awe-inspiring giant ponderosas. Given this wide geographic range and ecological diversity, it is difficult to imagine how a blanket, nationwide prescription for roadless area management can make any sense. The failure of RARE I and RARE II taught that it is not possible for decision-makers located in Washington, DC, to know with certainty the best prescription for every single roadless area. Yet the current DEIS and proposal do not even attempt to identify the most appropriate prescription for each roadless area. Instead, the proposal and most of the alternatives considered contemplate a single blanket prescription for all inventoried roadless areas outside of the Tongass Forest.

Why is a blanket prohibition on roadless areas appropriate?

The DEIS says that such a prescription is needed because:
- Road construction, reconstruction, and timber harvest activities in inventoried roadless and other unroaded areas can directly threaten their fundamental characteristics through the alteration of natural landscapes and fragmentation of forest lands;
- Budget constraints permit only a small portion of the agency road system to be effectively managed; and
- National concern over roadless area management continues to generate controversy, including costly and time-consuming appeals and litigation.

These statements may all be true, but they do not explain why a nationwide regulation is needed. One-size-fits-all prescriptions cannot recognize the different needs of the ecologically diverse National Forest System. Furthermore, regional and national forest managers are acutely aware of all of these considerations. Thus, given the right incentives, they are certain to take these factors into account when reevaluating roadless areas in forest planning. When planning on-the-ground projects, national forest officials and district rangers are more likely to find the best prescription for an individual roadless area than could be found in a three-and-one-half page rule written in Washington, DC.

The DEIS also makes such points as:
- Activities that pollute water "are minimal in roadless areas";
- Roadless areas "are often associated with healthier fish populations";
- "Many important wildlife populations are also heavily dependent on roadless areas";
- "Roadless areas are more likely to have intact native plant and animal communities"; and
- They provide "unique recreation opportunities".

These statements may be true, but they do not prove the need for a blanket national regulation. As with the previous claims, national forest and ranger district managers are fully aware of watershed, fish, wildlife, and recreation values. Moreover, even though these statements are often true, they are not necessarily true for every single roadless area in the National Forest System. It is easily possible that, in some roadless areas, a new road could enhance economic and social values by more than its environmental and economic cost.

Why now?

Of the 54 million acres of inventoried roadless areas, the forest plans of the 1980s placed 20.5 million acres in categories that forbid any road construction. Most forest plans were completed more than a decade ago, yet roads have been built in only 8 percent of the 33.8 million acres where roads are allowed. This indicates that roadless areas that are available for development have been developed at the rate of less than 1 percent per year.

A decline of less than 1 percent per year can be worrisome over the long term, but not over four or five years. Yet, even without the proposed policy, the future of all remaining roadless areas would be re-evaluated in the course of forest plan reviews that are scheduled to take place over the next four or five years.

During that time, the regional and national forest managers who are acutely aware of the environmental and social values of roadless areas, the cost of building and maintaining roads, and the controversies over road construction would have an opportunity to withdraw from potential development all roadless lands where road construction is inappropriate.

So why is a national blanket prescription against roads needed now? The DEIS says that "The national decision process would reduce the time, expense, and controversy associated with making case-by-case decisions at the local level." By the same logic, the federal government might as well tell every American what to eat to save them from the time, expense, and debate of having to make such decisions themselves. Naturally, everyone would be required to eat the same things even if some were diabetics and others were lactose intolerant.

Just as ordering everyone to eat exactly the same food could have dangerous and costly consequences for some people, applying the same prescription to all roadless areas carries a high risk that the results for some of the roadless areas will be wrong. While the construction of permanent roads may well be the wrong prescription for most roadless areas, the DEIS falls far short of providing enough information to justify a mandate that *all* roads should be excluded from *all* inventoried roadless areas. . . .

Will a blanket roadless policy protect ecosystem health?

The roadless area question is often portrayed by the media as pitting nature vs. development. In fact, many of the undeveloped roadless areas are just as unnatural today as the clearcuts that dot the National Forest System. While most roadless areas have never been roaded, logged, or mined, they are ecologically very different from the way they were when the Forest Service began managing them in 1905. Many who might have hiked through them a century ago would not recognize them today.

At least four factors have led to ecological changes within many of the roadless areas that are as significant as the road construction and clearcutting that has taken place outside of the roadless areas:

1. The Forest Service's fire suppression policy;
2. The removal, largely by federal agents, of large predators such as wolves and grizzly bear;
3. The introduction of exotic species such as plants and diseases; and
4. Roads and logging activities outside of the roadless areas, whose ecological effects often penetrate deep into the roadless areas.

The Forest Service's fire suppression policy has completely altered plant communities and wildlife habitat. People living in the 1920s could recall driving through the ponderosa pine forests of eastern Oregon and Washington or the mixed conifer forests of the Sierra Nevada. Now the vegetation is so thick that people have a hard time walking through them.

Natural and aboriginal fires played different roles and occurred with different frequencies in different forest types. In general, however, fires kept forest stocking levels down, favored some species of plants and animals over others, and minimized the highly flammable fine materials. Some trees, including giant sequoia and lodgepole pine, are fire dependent across much of their ranges, meaning that they rely on fire to germinate their seeds and suppress competition.

Fire suppression led to increased stocking of trees and vegetation. Trees that previously would have been killed by fire remained alive but lacked vigor due to competition from other vegetation. As a result, the weakened trees were susceptible to insect and disease problems. This sometimes led to insect epidemics spreading to other lands, both public and private.

Unless managers can build temporary roads to access and treat fuel build-ups in roadless areas, the cost of preventing fires may often be prohibitive.

Fire exclusion also led to major changes in species composition in many ecosystems. Species that were favored by fire lost out to other species that were previously less profuse. This sometimes created conditions for more insect problems as well as altered wildlife habitat.

Finally, fire suppression allowed a build up of flammable, fine materials. Increased stocking and increased numbers of insect-killed trees created a "ladder of fire" allowing fires on the forest floor quickly to become crown fires [in treetops]. Fires that previously might have been minor turned into catastrophic stand-killing fires.

In addition to fire suppression, roadless areas have been ecologically changed by the federal government's policy of removing large predators, such as wolves and grizzly bear, from much of the landscape. Another factor is the introduction of exotic species, often by federal actions such as the construction of roads along the boundaries of the roadless areas. In southwestern Oregon, for example, road construction is responsible for the spread of a non-native fungus that is killing most of the area's Port-Orford-cedar, which is the most valuable softwood in North America.

Wilderness vs. naturalness

To describe such areas as "natural," in the sense that they are uninfluenced by modern civilization, is factually incorrect. Roadless areas do continue to produce higher quality water than most roaded areas, but from a vegetation or wildlife viewpoint they have been completely transformed. Though they may be "wild," most roadless areas are far from natural.

Polls show that, given a choice between wilderness vs. high-impact roads and clearcutting, most Americans would choose wilderness. But it is not so clear that, given a choice between wildness and naturalness, most Americans would choose unnatural wildness.

For more than a decade, scientists and other professionals have debated the question of wilderness vs. naturalness. An area that is left alone may be described as *wild*. But certain management practices such as prescribed fires, pesticides to remove exotic plants, intensive hunting of selected species, and even selection cutting of timber will help more to make an area *natural*—that is, more like its pre-1900 condition—than leaving it alone. All of these practices could be aided by, and some may require, temporary low-impact roads that the proposed rule would prohibit.

The DEIS completely ignores this question. . . . In essence, the DEIS presents the over-simplified view that the debate is between nature vs. development.

The proposal to ban all roads in inventoried roadless areas outside of the Tongass National Forest merely exacerbates the problems caused by past policies such as fire suppression and predator removal. Due to those policies, future forest fires are more likely to become uncontrollable. Unless managers can build temporary roads to access and treat fuel build-ups in roadless areas, the cost of preventing fires may often be prohibitive.

Ecological restoration aimed at both reducing fire hazards and at restoring vegetation to something more closely resembling pre–Forest Service conditions may require a variety of tools, including thinnings, prescribed burnings, creation of openings, pesticides to kill exotic plants, and plantings to restore natural diversity. Any of these tools can be applied without temporary roads, but their cost will often be greater, which means that fewer areas will be restored.

According to . . . the DEIS, two-thirds or more of the roadless acres in Arizona, Montana, New Mexico, Oregon, South Dakota, and Washington are at "moderate to high risk of catastrophic fire," and a third or more of the roadless acres in Arizona, Nevada, New Mexico, Oregon, and Utah "need treatment" to reduce such fire hazards. The proposed roadless area rule will make such treatments more expensive, which means that the risk of more Los Alamos–like fires [in New Mexico] will be higher. The proposed roadless area rule allows road construction only "to protect public health and safety in cases of an imminent threat of flood, fire, or other catastrophic event." In other words, a road can be built to suppress a fire that should not have happened, but not to take the actions needed to prevent it. . . .

Roadless area conservation is deficient in several respects. It fails to show that a blanket, nationwide prescription is needed for roadless lands. It provides little data and what data it does provide indicate that a blanket, no-roads rule will cost more than it will benefit in at least some roadless areas. And it fails to consider important alternatives, including alternatives built around incentives rather than proscriptions, and alternatives that would allow temporary, low-impact roads in roadless areas when needed for forest health or ecosystem restoration.

Reflecting these deficiencies, the proposed rule will impose unnecessary economic and environmental costs on the national forests. The economic cost will be high because a ban on roads will increase the cost of improving forest health or restoring ecosystems in some roadless areas. The environmental cost will be high because, without such improvements, many roadless area ecosystems will continue to deteriorate and may even suffer unnaturally catastrophic fires.

These problems reflect several inadequacies with the roadless area rulemaking. First, the proposal is not based on science, and the ecological variety and unique needs of individual forests are ignored. Second, the proposal suffers from an inside-the-beltway mentality, which assumes that the only way to manage a 192-million acre estate is through central direction from the top down. Finally, the proposal ignores the important debate over wildness vs. naturalness.

There is no doubt that the Forest Service may have made many mistakes in the past, which may include building too many roads at too high an economic and environmental cost. But the roadless area rulemaking makes no attempt to identify the source of these mistakes. Instead, it simply attempts to preempt further mistakes at potentially high cost—the preemption of the construction of roads that might be necessary or useful for national forest management.

A roadless area rule is not the best way to prevent future errors. Instead, what is needed is a major reform of the Forest Service's budgetary process. Such a reform would improve management and reduce environmental and economic costs on all Forest Service lands whether or not they are designated as "roadless."

Short of such a major reform, the roadless area DEIS should consider an alternative that would ban permanent roads but allow temporary, low-impact roads in certain areas for forest health or ecosystem restoration. This would eliminate most of the objections to the proposed rule while retaining most, if not all, of the benefits.

5

The Government's Forest Policy Will Prevent Wildfires

George W. Bush

George W. Bush is the forty-third president of the United States. The Healthy Forests Initiative is one of the primary pieces of environmental legislation passed by his administration.

For the last fifty years, the U.S. Forest Service has suppressed nearly all wildfires in America's national forests. This practice is contrary to the natural process wherein small fires burn underbrush while allowing large trees to survive. This fire suppression has created a perilous situation in the American wilderness by allowing forests to become dangerously overgrown with small trees and bushes. During dry periods, this material has ignited into uncontrollable conflagrations, burning large trees, destroying property, and killing dozens of people. The Healthy Forest Restoration Act is a government program that finances the thinning of this underbrush through timber sales. This thinning in America's woodlands will build healthy forests through sound management practices.

Almost 750 million acres of forest stand, tall and beautiful across the 50 states. We have a responsibility to be good stewards of our forests. That's a solemn responsibility. . . . With the Healthy Forest Restoration Act we will help to prevent catastrophic wildfires, we'll help save lives and property, and we'll help protect our forests from sudden and needless destruction. . . .

For decades, government policies have allowed large amounts of underbrush and small trees to collect at the base of our forests. The motivations of this approach were good. But our failure to maintain the forests has had dangerous consequences and devastating consequences. The uncontrolled growth, left by years of neglect chokes off nutrients from trees and provides a breeding ground for insects and disease.

As we have seen [in 2003] and in other years, such policy creates the conditions for devastating wildfires. Today, about 190 million acres of forest and woodlands around the country are vulnerable to destruction. Over-

George W. Bush, statement made upon signing the Healthy Forests Initiative into law, Washington, DC, December 3, 2003.

38

grown brush and trees can serve as kindling, turning small fires into large, raging blazes that burn with such intensity that the trees literally explode.

I saw that firsthand when we were flying over Oregon, magnificent trees just exploding as we choppered by. The resulting devastation damages the habitats of endangered species, causes flooding and soil erosion, harms air quality, oftentimes ruins water supplies. These catastrophic fires destroy homes and businesses; they put lives at risk, especially the lives of the brave men and women who are on the front line of fighting these fires.

Tragic consequences

In two years' time, fires throughout the country have burned nearly 11 million acres. We've seen the cost that wildfires bring, in the loss of 28 firefighters [in 2003] alone. In the fires that burned across Southern California this fall, 22 civilians also lost their lives, as whole neighborhoods vanished into flames. . . .

Overgrown brush and trees can serve as kindling, turning small fires into large, raging blazes that burn with such intensity that the trees literally explode.

We're seeing the tragic consequences brought by years of unwise forest policy. We face a major national challenge, and we're acting together to solve the challenge. The Healthy Forest Initiative I announced [in 2002] marked a clear and decisive change in direction. Instead of enduring season after season of devastating fires, my administration acted to remove the causes of severe wildfires. We worked within our existing legal authority to thin out and remove forest undergrowth before disaster struck. We emphasized thinning projects in critical areas. And since the beginning of 2002, we've restored almost 5 million acres of overgrown forest and rangeland.

And that's pretty good progress. But it's not enough progress. And so, thanks to . . . the Healthy Forest Restoration Act . . . we now can expand the work to a greater scale that the dangers of wildfires demand. . . .

The bill expedites the environmental review process so we can move forward more quickly on projects that restore forests to good health. We don't want our intentions bogged down by regulations. We want to get moving. When we see a problem, this government needs to be able to move. Congress wisely enabled a review process to go forward, but also wisely recognizes sometimes review process bogs us down and things just don't get done.

The new law directs courts to consider the long-term risks that could result if thinning projects are delayed. And that's an important reform. . . . It places reasonable time limits on litigation after the public has had an opportunity to comment and a decision has been made. You see, no longer will essential forest health projects be delayed by lawsuits that drag on year after year after year.

High standards of stewardship

This Act of Congress sets the right priorities for the management of our nation's forests, focusing on woodlands that are closest to communities and on places where the risk to wildlife and the environment is the greatest. It enforces high standards of stewardship so that we can ensure that we're returning our forests to more natural conditions and maintaining a full range of forest types. It enables collaboration between community groups and private stewardship organizations and all levels of government before projects are chosen. This law will not prevent every fire, but it is an important step forward, a vital step to make sure we do our duty to protect our nation's forests.

The principles behind the Healthy Forest Initiative were not invented in the White House, and truthfully, not invented in the Congress. They are founded on the experience of scientists, forestry experts, and, as importantly, the firefighters who know what they're talking about. Chief Tom O'Keefe, of the California Department of Forestry, is among those who have seen the consequences of misguided forest policy. He put it this way: "A lot of people have been well-intentioned. They saved trees, but they lost the forest." We want to save the forests.

This bill was passed because members of Congress looked at sound science, did the best they could to get all the politics out of the way for good legislation. Members from both parties came together, people from different regions of the country. A broad range of people who care about our forests were listened to, whether they be conservationists, or resource managers, people from the South, people from the West, people from New York. You see, we share duties of stewardship. And today we shared in an important accomplishment.

6

The Government's Forest Policy Is Destructive

Matthew Hall and Lokiko Hall

Matthew Hall is a forester who logs forests using traditional methods such as horses and axes. He is also a teacher of ecological forestry at the Aprovecho Research Institute in Cottage Grove, Oregon. Lokiko Hall is a journalist and founder of Bummers & Gummers, *a journal of country life.*

The Healthy Forests Initiative signed into law by President Bush calls for the supression of forest fires through the removal of underbrush and small trees. It also allows for the sale of old-growth trees as a way to finance the thinning process. Instead of financing underbrush removal with timber sales of mature trees, the government should make it profitable for sawmills to sell wood cut from the underbrush. These thin trees, called small roundwood, can be used in various aspects of construction such as fencing and sheds. Currently small roundwood cannot be marketed because government lumber inspectors have no way to grade these small poles as usable lumber. If a new method of lumber grading were instituted, the sale of small roundwood would be profitable and rare old-growth forests could be preserved as national treasures for future generations.

Fire was a key component of the management strategy of Western Indians. Their villages and communities were kept safe from wildfire by prescribed burning that kept the landscape clear of dry grass, brush and small trees. Historical evidence shows there was much more open prairie around the valleys and foothills and less forest than there is currently. Periodic wildfires swept through the forested areas and shaped the old-growth forest, the remnants of which we see today. The Kalapuya [of northwest Oregon] were reputed to grow their tobacco in burned clearings in the forest where there were large burned logs on the ground. The tribes who lived in the Cascades frequently burned under the Ponderosa Pine forest to keep the understory open and clear of brush species and regenerating conifers.

Since the Native Americans were prevented from burning 150 to 160 years ago, and since our emphasis has been to suppress wildfires, fuel levels have built up to catastrophic levels. Fire is a natural occurrence in the West. The question in any particular area is not will it burn, but what is the expected interval between fires. The south hills of Eugene [Oregon], for instance, should expect to experience small fires every 35 to 50 years, whereas the Olympic Peninsula [in Washington State] might experience fire in the form of a massive conflagration every 1,000 years.

A century and a half later, we are just beginning to admit to what the natives always knew: that fire must be fought with fire and that small, low-intensity fires will for the most part prevent big fires. But we still have a ways to go insofar as living within the limits of our environment and understanding that there are some things we should not try to control.

During the devastating wildfires of summer 2002 more than seven million acres burned. This prompted President Bush to draft his Healthy Forest Initiative [that he signed into law as The Healthy Forest Restoration Act in December 2003]. It is estimated that 190 million acres of public land need to be thinned and managed to reduce high levels of accumulated fuels. Ninety-eight million acres of private and state lands are at risk of catastrophic fire. I agree with this much, more or less.

I have been a working forester for over 20 years, with experience in England, Northern Ireland, and the states of Washington, California, and Oregon. I am primarily interested in promoting sustainable forestry—and in doing the research to discover what that actually is. Thinning and fuel reduction, prescribed burning and wildland fires must be a part of any sustainable forestry system we eventually devise. Please be wary of glib statements by industry, government, or even environmentalists.

Sustainability means forever and covers many aspects: forests, communities, wildlife, soil, water—whole ecosystems. We may not know enough yet to accurately define this sustainable model, and we may not be willing to accept what a sustainable demand upon resources will turn out to be. When the initiative was first announced, I thought, Great! The government is actually going to get out there, spend some money in the rural communities, and thin its overstocked forests. My optimism was short-lived.

The need to thin forests

I acquired a copy of the "Healthy Forest: An Initiative for Wildfire Prevention and Stronger Communities." The "executive statement" of this many-branched trail of paper and internet sites stresses the need for fuels reduction, and argues that citizen and environmental lawsuits are to blame for gridlocking these essential projects. It finished with five paragraphs entitled "Fulfilling the promise of the 1994 Northwest Forest Plan." Aha! I thought, here we have the crux of the matter. Because of procedural and judicial delays, agencies were only able to offer for sale less than 40% of the planned timber volume in 2001—much less than what was offered in the NW Forest Plan.

Here's a quote from that section: "The projected sustainable timber supply has failed to materialize, and the fire prone areas of the forest are unhealthier now than before the plan existed." Now what does timber production have to do with hazardous fuel reduction projects? Timber harvesting, and the accompanying road construction projects, would seem to increase hazardous fuel buildup and human caused fires.

In the environmental impact research from the development of the Roadless [Area Conservation] Rule [a federal rule that protects forests from logging practices], the Forest Service found that fires are twice as likely to occur in previously roaded and logged areas than in large road-less areas. Timber harvesting and hazardous fuel reduction activities are two completely different things. Timber harvests and timber sales are intended to produce a commercial product, usually sawlogs for the making of dimension lumber. Timber harvests are achieved by thinning (occasionally) or by clearcutting (usually, but perhaps with a clever name like "regeneration harvest").

Hazardous fuel reduction is by thinning dense thickets of young conifer trees, brush and shrubs. Often material is slashed to the ground and left. Thinning may be followed by a prescribed burn. This would clean up the tangle of tiny trunks lying every which way on the forest floor. So the objectives of the Healthy Forest Initiative are two-fold: to reduce hazardous fuel buildups and to restore the timber supply promised in the Northwest Forest Plan. I learned that these things are to be accomplished by simply removing the threat of lawsuits by environmentalists (or anyone else).

This is to be done by making *categorical exclusions:* something for which the president does not need to seek congressional approval. During the fire season of 2002 a Forest Service spokesperson stated on the radio that environmentalists were stalling fuel reduction thinnings with lawsuits and that this was why the forests were burning. Now what the Sierra Club says is "Projects to protect communities are not controversial. We haven't appealed or tried to delay community protections measures, and we won't." Furthermore, the Government Accounting Office reported in August 2001 that out of 1,671 hazardous fuel reduction projects in fiscal year 2001, only 20 had been appealed and none had been litigated.

The Bush Administration, however, didn't like this study and came up with one of its own which found that (surprise!) 48% of projects were appealed and 20% went into litigation. According to Environmental Media Services, the Bush study focused on only 326 projects, most of which were timber sales that did not qualify for the congressional fuels reduction fund.

An excuse to harvest old-growth forests

Anyone in the forests products industry knows that fuel reduction thinning, pre-commercial thinning and early commercial thinning are operations that have to be paid for. Smaller trees have never been desired by mills because they can't make 2x4s or plywood out of them, thus in the past many thinning operations were completely paid for by the government. But that was also because in the past not so much thinning was needed. All the way up into the 1970s, most logging that took place was the liquidation of forests that had grown under the influence of periodic fires. Nowadays, though, fire suppression efforts have made it so that we can't expect decent timber to be created through time and fire. So now we have to spend money doing non-commercial management of regrowth in order to create future valuable lumber. The government, if it is to follow sound business practices, needs to sell its timber for a big enough profit to pay for these treatments.

But the government has not adjusted to the new situation that its own policies have created. It has now developed so many overstocked forests that it can't afford the massive outlay needed to hire private companies to correct this mess. According to Assistant Secretary of the Interior Rebecca Watson, "This kind of subsidy is just [impractical]." But that doesn't change the fact that currently no one in the real world expects to produce a commercial product from these operations.

This, though, is exactly what the government hopes for and hints at in its Initiative. There is a murky reference in the Executive Statement to "funding for . . . market utilization of small diameter materials [trees]"; however, Ms. Watson, said in an interview while in Montana, that creating a market for small, spindly trees is not one of the pillars of the Forest Initiative. Instead the government will promise to supply the stuff virtually ad infinitum with the hope that the private sector, given a new, cheap resource, will make some commercially valuable use for it.

Because the government does not want to pay for these overdue, underfunded, and neglected projects, it will trade timber harvests (quality stuff now) as a form of payment for the noncommercial operations. How it intends to do this goes something like this: Under the proposed legislation, hazardous fuel reduction activities, and activities for rehabilitating and stabilizing land and infrastructure impacted by wildland fires or fire suppression would become "categorical exclusions," i.e., they don't require further analysis in either an environmental assessment or an environmental impact statement (EIS). As things stand now, if there is no EIS, people can't appeal.

The Healthy Forest Initiative . . . is a backdoor means to higher levels of timber harvesting. . . . A likely excuse to harvest mature forests.

Accordingly, this legislation "would not include activities such as timber sales that do not have hazardous fuel reduction as their primary purpose." So the government's primary purpose is to undertake hazardous fuel reduction activities on these lands; its secondary purpose is to attach timber sales to these projects to provide the money to pay for the primary objective. This is the reason that so many environmental groups are opposing the Healthy Forest Initiative. It is a backdoor means to higher levels of timber harvesting. In particular, a likely excuse to harvest mature forests.

If the government is going to trade timber sales as payment for hazardous fuel reduction projects this is a bad time to do it. Lumber supply currently exceeds demand, so log prices are low. Since 1997 prices have been around 10% less than 10 years ago, and 30% to 40% less than the boom period of 1992–1996. After the glut of timber created by the February 2002 windstorm, I had trouble finding anyone at all who wanted to buy a load of logs in Fall 2002. (That was, however, a localized glut as everyone scrambled to salvage logs from landowners who hadn't even been contemplating harvesting their trees.) The main reason why timber prices are so low—despite record demand for lumber—is that cheap imports have been flooding in from Canada and Eastern Europe. Selling off timber at low prices means that we can treat fewer acres for fuel reductions with the money or trade that is earned. It would make more sense to spend what funds are available on priority areas now and hold back timber sales as a source of income when the economy picks up and we have used up our oversupply of logs and lumber—and when other countries are no longer dumping cheap wood into our markets.

As it stands, though, the sawmills and timber companies will be happy to buy massive quantities of high-quality logs cheap. They can be stockpiled and sawn at a future date. In particular old-growth logs will last for many years without rotting, This couldn't be a better deal for the timber companies; they will get to buy low and sell high—in the tradition of the finest of business practices.

A little market analysis

Let us step back from the rhetoric and look at what needs to be done.

I agree there are millions of acres in the Western Forests that need thinning and clearing of brush species. I agree that currently these activities must be paid for as there is little or no commercial market for the little trees, saplings and brush that need to be cut down and disposed of in some manner. Now if the existing dense tree and brush growth is a result of regrowth after timber harvesting on government land, then it would make sense that the government agency involved should have set aside some of the money earned from timber harvesting to pay for the necessary work to fireproof and thin. When we've all stopped laughing, we should remember that the Forest Service and other government agencies are mandated to produce a sustained volume of timber.

To do this management it is required to bring regrowth into a productive capacity. This shouldn't have come as such a big surprise to the government. The timber companies work such practices into their cost accounting when they manage the forests that they own outright. Other activities such as pre-commercial thinning and early commercial thinning could create commercial products if the necessary research is done— for instance stress grading small roundwood for building material. But at this time there is no system in place for determining the strength and value of small diameter poles.

Utilize small wood

All lumber coming out of sawmill is graded and stamped according to its quality. Only lumber of certain grades can be used in framing coded buildings, i.e., grades of #2 or better, and *every piece* of structural wood must have a stamp on it. But if a person or construction outfit wants to use poles in a building project these poles must also be graded somehow. However, currently lumber graders can only stamp lumber that has four flat sides.

In order to grade poles, a lumber grader writes out a certificate describing the poles individually, obviously a more expensive and time-consuming process than giving each piece the appropriate stamp. For small diameter poles to be widely used in construction some new grading rules would have to be developed. Probably these would be based on the width of the pole and the number of growth rings per inch of diameter. The pole itself would be stamped to indicate its comparative strength as dimensional lumber, e.g. the equivalent to a Number One 2 × 4, etc. Creating a viable commercial product from small roundwood would be a way to reduce the cost of these operations and make them more financially self-sufficient; it would also help private industry.

Of course, the public would have to be encouraged to buy the product—perhaps they would if it was marketed as a hazardous-fuel-reduction product. This would make such poles one of the few wood products you could buy that will let you feel that you are making forests healthier by your consumption of lumber. Until this is done, the only markets for this small roundwood are for chips for pulpwood or to a fence post manufacturer. . . . Chip prices have been low for years. . . . Prices make it difficult to supply these markets and make back the expenses of thinning (much less any sort of profit), especially if long trucking distances are involved.

I have memories of contractors working first thinning operations in England in the late '70s. Many of them went broke because the profit margin in supplying pulpwood and fence posts wasn't sufficient to keep them solvent. Currently pre-commercial thinning is done in both public and private forestry as an investment costing between $60–$120 per acre. It is used as a management tool to encourage the forest to grow faster and to avoid doing a first thinning that might not pay for itself at today's chip prices.

Creating a viable commercial product from small roundwood would be a way to reduce the cost of [thinning] operations and make them more financially self-sufficient.

Pre-commercial thinning provides similar benefits to hazardous fuel reduction projects. Trees are thinned out to wider spacing by removing dead and dying trees that tend to accumulate under thicket conditions. Creating a viable market for small roundwood could reduce the cost to the landowner (or taxpayer) of pre-commercial or early thinnings.

Making homes safer

Let us return to the topic of fuel reduction. Many people have moved from the city and suburbs out to lovely wooded properties in the countryside around our rural towns, for instance around Bend, Redmond and Sisters [Oregon]. This development of the countryside places houses out into very fire-prone areas. Consequently, much money and sometimes lives are lost defending these properties from the fires that inevitably come. From what I've seen, these people often like the privacy offered by thickets of trees around their houses. This is the first place to start fuel reduction. Landowners in these places need to do serious hazardous fuels reduction to create firebreaks around their properties.

Experience from previous fire-fighting efforts show that when a fire enters an area that has been treated for hazardous fuel reduction it is much easier to get under control than in untreated areas. Furthermore firefighters at the Los Alamos fire of (2001) mentioned going onto private property that was infested with doghair (short spindly trees perfect for burning) and that many homes had needles and branches on their roofs. Obviously making these places safer will require education and probably some sort of government subsidies like the cost-share programs now available to private landowners for other sorts of restoration work. These areas are closer to potential markets than backcountry projects and therefore any wood products coming from these operations would have more chance of being commercially viable. This would help offset the costs of this work, which are going to be enormous.

Because everyone is worried about fire, it is a cheap shot to combine hazardous fuel reduction with logging of old growth.

The Sierra Club estimates in its own 22-page healthy forest plan that creating 500-yard-wide "community protection zones" around rural towns and properties in the west would cost $2 billion a year for a minimum of five years. However it should be noted that land within 100 to 200 feet of structures is the most important area for fuel reduction. Furthermore, clearance past this zone did not seem to affect the occurrence of house ignitions.

One might ask why the government should subsidize this work on private land. The easy answer is that hazardous fuel reduction projects are cheaper than fighting fires. Once these areas are treated, and made defensible, fuel reduction projects could move out toward the back country. The further out we get from markets the less likely it will be that commercial products will be viable without subsidies of one sort or another. That raises the question of where does the money come from? As far as timber harvesting goes there are two kinds of projects that are very commercially viable.

The first is harvesting mature forest (old growth), the second is thinning older second (regrowth of lands cut over in the '50s, '60s, and '70s). Mature forest is now, of course, such a rare commodity that it should all be preserved, preferably with surrounding regrowth areas set aside as late successional reserve, if for nothing else than as habitat for threatened and endangered species.

However, there are large tracts of maturing second growth that can be thinned at a profit. *Thinned* at a profit; they don't need to be clearcut. If any timber has to be harvested to pay for hazardous fuel reduction projects, I would like to hope that it will be from second growth forests that actually need thinning.

Well, that's probably not going to happen, because we all know that this forest plan is just a sexy way to ramp up logging. If a compromise were ever possible on this, then the following is what I would suggest: Use available funding to do hazardous fuel reduction projects in forest areas adjacent to communities first, These projects could be excluded from environmental impact statements (EIS), if absolutely necessary. As these projects are almost never contested, an EIS is not needed to allow for appeal.

Further, this would speed up their process considerably. But timber sales should not be tagged onto these projects and slid in under the same exclusion. It's important that the professionals that the Forest Service employs go out and look for endangered species before they log mature timber.

Because everyone is worried about fire, it is a cheap shot to combine hazardous fuel reduction with logging of old growth, particularly in this way. The Healthy Forest Initiative removes the environmental scoping that is important on timber sales. Without this scoping and cataloging of species, we won't know what is there that we need to protect.

7

Oil Drilling Will Ruin the Wilderness Character of the Arctic National Wildlife Refuge

Susan McGrath

Susan McGrath was the environmental columnist for the Seattle Times *for eight years and currently writes articles about the environment for* Audubon *and other magazines.*

One of the largest areas of untouched wilderness left in the United States can be found in the Arctic National Wildlife Refuge (ANWR) in northern Alaska. While winter snows and extreme cold leave this area barren most of the year, in the warm summer months it is an important habitat for birds, caribou, moose, and endangered species such as grizzly bears and polar bears. ANWR also lies atop a huge pool of underground oil. While politicians and oil companies are eager to drill in ANWR, the total estimated amount of petroleum there would only satisfy the oil needs of the United States for six to twenty months. This short-term fix to America's energy needs is a poor way to manage the Arctic wilderness. The United States uses 25 percent of the world's oil and only has about 5 percent of the world's reserves, although the prodrilling lobby refuses to admit this fact. Drilling in ANWR is not going to change this disproportionate use of resources. Protection of the wildlife in ANWR should take precedence over the short-sighted needs of powerful oil companies and a Congress that refuses to require automakers to improve gas mileage on trucks and cars.

The Arctic sun lies low in the west, slanting shadows long across the gravel bars. The Aichilik River meanders around us in a dozen shallow channels. From here, the serried mountains and foothills of the Brooks Range fan out across the horizon. . . .

The three of us are on a midnight ramble, coursing the chilly tundra like 10-year-olds allowed to stay out past bedtime on a summer night, exhilarated by the midnight sun. We flush a willow ptarmigan. It is still in winter white, though it's almost two days past the solstice and the snow is gone from the flat places. "Male," notes Andy. "The female will already be in summer plumage, on the nest. He takes the heat, distracts the predators." We search for the female in the leafless willows at our feet. But if she's here, her camouflage defeats us. Abandoning the search, Dave bounds up the fluted snowbank; Andy and I crest the rise in time to see him belly flop onto the cottongrass tussocks, and we instinctively follow suit. There, approaching fast across the tundra, are three caribou cows and two small calves. We hold our breath.

These are caribou of the Porcupine herd, a migratory population of 129,000 named for a tributary of the Yukon River. The herd winters along the river on the south slope of the Brooks Range, and east into Canada. Come spring, the animals migrate across the passes, then north and west onto the coastal plain. For four to seven weeks the cows fatten their calves here, finding a rare combination of high-quality vegetation and relatively few predators. They fatten despite the fact that they also encounter mosquitoes and parasites by the maddening trillions. The insects goad the animals into tight herds, tens of thousands thick. . . .

This year spring is cold and late. There's not a mosquito or warble fly in sight, and the caribou are dribbling onto the tundra in modest pulses. Even so, there is something about them—the purposefulness of the adults, the sturdiness and vigor of the little ones—that is intensely affecting.

The animals trot past us and descend to the river gravel. Halfway across the strand, an arctic tern launches an aerial attack. The terns lay their eggs in the gravel, and the caribou have strayed too near a nest. As we watch, wincing, the bird dive-bombs the lead cow in a merciless series of strikes. The caribou buck and wheel, running 25 yards upstream before plunging into the channel and crossing the river to the tundra on the other side.

Centerpiece of the Bush energy plan

Animals know no political boundaries, of course, and one side of the river looks much like the other. But in crossing the Aichilik, the caribou have moved onto what is possibly the most hotly and long-contested piece of real estate in America: the coastal plain of the Arctic National Wildlife Refuge [ANWR].

For the past three decades, pro-development groups and Alaska's powerful congressional delegation have pushed hard to open the plain to oil exploration. Environmentalists, including groups such as the Audubon Society, have pushed back. In 1989 Congress seemed close to approving drilling when the [oil tanker] *Exxon Valdez* spilled 11 million gallons of crude oil into Alaska's Prince William Sound. The bill was quietly shelved.

Today President George W. Bush, backed by many members of Congress, has made drilling in the refuge a centerpiece of his energy plan. On August 1 [2003] the House of Representatives approved a bill based on that plan; it calls for oil and gas drilling in the coastal plain. The Senate will begin work on its energy package this fall. Though drilling faces much more opposition in that chamber, Perry Plumart, Audubon's director of government relations, says, "The Senate is the last bastion. If for whatever reason it passes the Senate, then there's drilling in the refuge." [Editor's note: The bill did not pass in the Senate.] Lois J. Schiffer, Audubon's senior vice-president for public policy, called the House vote "a catastrophe for the environment" and urged the Senate to counter it. But Secretary of the Interior Gale Norton had already indicated the administration would not back down, telling the Associated Press in June, "This is an issue that has been debated for the last quarter-century. I imagine we will continue to talk about it no matter what Congress does or doesn't do this year."

The caribou have moved onto what is possibly the most hotly and long-contested piece of real estate in America: the coastal plain of the Arctic National Wildlife Refuge.

Bob Marshall started it. A radical thinker who worked for the U.S. Forest Service in the 1920s and went on to cofound the Wilderness Society, he wrote, "In the name of a balanced use of American resources, let's keep Alaska largely a wilderness?" His ideas, even more inflammatory then than now, inspired the early visionaries of the Alaska environmental movement. Calling northeast Alaska "The Last Great Wilderness," they articulated a philosophy in which wilderness was valued not just by scientific measures but for its aesthetic, even spiritual, worth. Roger Kaye, a 20-year veteran of the U.S. Fish and Wildlife Service and unofficial historian for the refuge, credits their work with helping make northeast Alaska "a symbolic landscape of national significance."

In 1960 that work culminated in President Eisenhower's protecting 8.9 million acres of the Brooks Range as the Arctic National Wildlife Range. Twenty years later the state, the federal government, and native Alaskans negotiated a giant land shuffle to clarify ownership and to set aside protected lands. The result was the Alaska National Interest Lands Conservation Act, or ANILCA, under which the area was renamed the Arctic National Wildlife Refuge and expanded to 19.5 million acres—bigger than South Carolina.

The refuge is unique, according to John Schoen, senior scientist with Audubon Alaska, for its geographical compression and the diversity of its ecoregions. "Here in the northeast corner of Alaska," he says, "you can travel 250 miles and cross all the ecoregions of the Arctic—boreal forest, forest tundra, mountains, arctic tundra, and coastal marine." In the book *Arctic Refuge: A Circle of Testimony*, Schoen wrote of an "immense country with large carnivores and their prey interacting as they have for millennia." The refuge, he pointed out, "represents a complete and functional ecosystem on a vast scale, unusual even for Alaska, and largely lost from the rest of the country."

Much of the refuge's mountain terrain—most of the original 8.9 million acres—was officially designated a wilderness area, a status conferring the most stringent protection. But protecting the refuge's coastal plain, a narrow band 15 to 40 miles wide, has been another matter entirely.

In 1968 the largest pool of oil ever found in North America was discovered under the broad coastal plain west of the refuge, at Prudhoe Bay. Since then oil companies have pumped more than 13 billion barrels of oil from that area, sending it south through the Trans-Alaska Pipeline to ships at Valdez. Evidence suggested the refuge's 1.5-million-acre coastal plain might contain reservoirs of oil, too. (Current estimates by the U.S. Geological Survey range from 4.25 billion to 11.8 billion barrels, a 6- to 20-month supply for the United States.) In a compromise move, Section 1002 of ANILCA placed the coastal plain in a special category for further review of both oil and wildlife "values." The fragile band of tundra has been known by the unlovely name of "the ten-oh-two" ever since.

America's largest mammals at play

"The moment Bush was confirmed, my phone started ringing off the hook with folks saying, 'Sign me up, I want to see the place before it's gone,'" Dave van den Berg told me. His company, Arctic Wild, guides trips into the refuge. I called him late. He had just one opening left—in June, the best month for seeing masses of caribou. The trip he offered would combine a leisurely paddle down the Aichilik, a typical braided Arctic river that delineates the eastern border of the 1002, with a few other stops, including a day trip to the oil fields at Prudhoe Bay.

Four months later, bundled into as many layers of petroleum-derived synthetic long underwear as a person could reasonably function in, 10 of us—guide Jennifer van den Berg, 8 other guests, and I—were delivered in shifts by bush plane to a barely perceptible landing strip in the treeless foothills of the North Slope. There we met guide Andy Elsberg and a lean and grizzled Dave, hot off a previous trip. We sorted ourselves into three rafts and set off placidly downstream. It was already late in the day, but night wouldn't fall for six weeks. We would gradually drift into what Dave calls "Arctic time": Dinner at midnight. Hiking at 2 A.M. Even a little paddling between 1 A.M. and 4. We would be picked up again by bush plane eight days and 45 miles later on a barrier island in the Beaufort Sea. Eight Arctic days: 192 hours of sunlight on a vast and spacious land.

> *"You can travel 250 miles and cross all the ecoregions of the Arctic—boreal forest, forest tundra, mountains, arctic tundra, and coastal marine."*

So spacious as to be almost overwhelming, I soon discovered. Latitude has stripped the tundra bare of trees, leaving only a waterlogged mantle of moss, sedge, and diminutive wildflowers, none much more than four inches high. The low vegetation and perennial daylight give the visitor an excellent chance of actually seeing North America's largest mammals at work and play—moose, wolf, musk ox, caribou, and all three species of the continent's bears: black, brown (also called grizzly), and polar.

We floated just a mile downriver before setting up camp that first night. Twenty minutes on, a grizzly slouched past us with a nearsighted air. The bear's tawny coat so precisely matched the still-brown vegetation that you could almost imagine it greening up as summer advanced and breaking out in patches of pink and yellow. When a metallic clink betrayed our presence, the bear gave a startled shake and padded rapidly away, casting sidelong glances both curious and shy. Not an hour later, two bull moose sauntered out from the same direction. They, too, started, then glided away at a leggy trot.

In the morning we saw our first caribou, an intermittent rivulet of cream and tan moving steadily north and west. Caribou are not the most elegant of deer. Their antlers are gawky, their snowshoe hooves reminiscent of Dr. Seuss. At this time of year they are shedding their winter coats in great clumps of hair, which gives them a shabby, moth-eaten look. What they lack in grace, though, they make up in stature, principally because of their large numbers. Their feces fertilize the soil, and they themselves are an important food source for predators.

The caribou are a month late in arriving on the coastal plain this year, delayed by deeper-than-average snow along the migration route. Last year's migration was late, too, with disastrous results. Some cows gave birth en route to the calving grounds. "Calves that usually get a free ride in mama's belly all the way to the coastal plain were having to struggle through snow and swim swollen torrents," says Fran Mauer, an Arctic Refuge biologist. "You'd see these wobbly little calves trying to keep up with their mothers, who were trying to keep up with the herd." Many calves drowned crossing the streams. Others were left behind by their mothers, the migratory urge even more powerful than the maternal. Experts estimate that almost half of the year's crop, some 15,000 calves, died in the first month of last year's calving season. So far this year, they have fared slightly better.

Vulnerable animals on the tundra

The effect of drilling on the long-term health of the Porcupine herd is of major concern to wildlife biologists. The central-Arctic herd at Prudhoe Bay has grown fivefold since that area was developed for oil, much to the delight of the oil industry. But biologists such as Mauer say the boom is misleading: Caribou numbers were low when development began, perhaps because of years of severe weather. A closer study of that herd by state biologists during the 1980s and 1990s showed that the concentration of calving shifted away from industrial sites to alternative calving grounds with less forage.

The Porcupine herd, here in the refuge, is almost five times bigger, but it calves in the same amount of acreage. Oil development could push animals to calve closer to the mountains, where there is poorer forage and a higher density of predators such as grizzly bears, wolves, and eagles. "This herd definitely seems less resilient," concludes Mauer.

Caribou aren't the only vulnerable animals on the tundra. The coastal plain is the most important terrestrial denning ground for polar bears along the entire 500-mile coast of the Beaufort Sea. Scientists worry that industrial activity will prompt mother bears to abandon their dens early, endangering their cubs. Some 250 musk oxen also live on the plain year-round, conserving energy in the harsh weather by moving very little. Disturb them and they stampede, wasting critical reserves. And other animals? A paper in the April issue of the journal *Conservation Biology* reviewed the scientific literature: In five decades of wildlife studies in the refuge, 44 percent focused on caribou, 16 percent on musk oxen, and 14 percent on polar bears. Of the other species that make this vast ecosystem their home, little is known.

Those first days of the trip, I was too enraptured by the big mammals and the big sky to admire the ground underfoot. Eventually, my gaze lowered. Centuries of freeze and thaw atop the permafrost have created arrangements of soil, silt, pebble, and stone that geologists call patterned ground. E.C. Pielou's *A Naturalist's Guide to the Arctic* lists almost as many names for tundra formations as Eskimos are said to have for snow: polygons, pingos, string bogs, frost boils, flarks, thermokarst, thaw slumps, sorted circles, stone stripes, palsas, and peat mounds.

Paddylike polygons fracture the flat ground for miles on either side of the river. These are an exaggerated version of the polygonal cracks you see in the mud of a dried puddle, cloaked in sedges and moss. A single polygon might measure anywhere from 5 to 50 yards in diameter. From the air, they cover the tundra in a green-brown mosaic.

The plushness of the low vegetation is deceiving. These are among the harshest conditions on earth for plants. Extreme cold, a short growing season, frost heaves, ferocious winds, drought conditions, a shallow root zone over the permafrost, and infertile soil conspire against plant life. Most years, plants are unable to set seeds, relying on vegetative propagation to reproduce. And they grow very slowly. When the ground is disturbed in this part of the world, it may not recover for decades.

"Oil-rig technology touted by President Bush as environmentally friendly and central to his expanded drilling plans has malfunctioned at rising rates in the past five years."

As our boats approached the coast, we crossed some imperceptible ecological boundary, though the landscape remained essentially unchanged. Every hour brought new waterfowl: tundra swans, eiders, redthroated loons, yellow-billed loons, Pacific loons, pintails, scaup, long-tailed ducks, and phalaropes. Finally, the river decanted us into the Beaufort Lagoon. Here we beached our rafts a final time on an unnamed barrier island—a mere swipe of gray-brown sand. The pack ice lay some quarter-mile off the seaward side of the island, bleak and quintessentially Arctic-looking.

The chilly open water between island and ice was speckled with waterfowl. Ninety-five bird species from 5 continents and 49 U.S. states migrate to this coastal plain. They come from the tropics, from the temperate zones. The arctic tern, champion migrant, comes all the way from Antarctica—10,000 miles. They have 6 or 8 or 10 short weeks to raise their young before they all make the trip back to their wintering grounds. Why do they come to this remote and barren-looking place? What could possibly be worth such a risky and extravagant journey?

The answer lay in a puddle. Tim Buckley, a high school science teacher along on a training grant, seined tiny creatures from it, cupping them in his palm. "These little shrimplike things are the first-level consumers," he said. "Zooplankton. They eat the phytoplankton.

"The big key is all this sunlight. If you're a little phytoplankton, you just need a few photons to get kicking. The sunlight is strong enough to penetrate a meter of ice, so algae attaches itself to the bottom of the ice, because that's as close as it can get to the sun. I spent a summer on an ice-breaker with a roving submersible, and we saw the ice algae—greenish-gold, almost translucent material hanging down under the ice. So the zoo-plankton eat the algae, and little fish eat the zooplankton—so do bowhead whales, for that matter—and now you've got a food chain going.

"It looks so barren, but this is one of the richest sources of food at this time of year. The Arctic is the only place that you're going to get these kinds of feeding opportunities."

Tim rocked back on his heels. "The thing you can't escape when you're talking about oil up here is: What the hell would you do if something ever went wrong? You could never clean it up. This place would never recover. Prudhoe Bay is very impressive, but that whole area will never be the same. It'll never recover from the kind of land transformation that's gone on there."

The largest industrial facility in the world

Prudhoe Bay is impressive. After eight days on the Aichilik it felt like the set of a science fiction movie. Eight hundred square miles of pipes and gravel pits and giant rectangular boxes and immaculate gravel roads and towering production facilities and operation centers and airports and workers in identical blue coveralls. The largest industrial facility in the world. Seeing it superimposed on the tundra polygons, their soft geometry still visible between the gravel pads and roads, was a little like seeing a bear at the zoo after watching one in the wild. The polygons were there, but their fierce, mysterious beauty was gone.

BP and Phillips Petroleum are the principal oil companies up here now. Though their track record is not perfect, under pressure from the environmental community they have made significant improvements over the years, shrinking the size of the equipment needed for each production facility. Nevertheless, the equipment needed even to survey for oil is mind-boggling in its scale. The May issue of *Scientific American* offers this list of equipment that oil companies would likely use to survey the 1002 the first winter after opening: "eight vibrating and seven recording vehicles, accompanied by personnel carriers, mechanic trucks, mobile shop trucks, fuel tankers, an incinerator, plus a crew of 80 to 120 people and a camp train of 20 to 25 shipping containers on skis, pulled by several Caterpillar tractors on treads."

The crew would drive up and down and back and forth across the entire coastal plain, leaving a grid of tracks in the tundra, boxes about 1,100 feet square. Each oil company would conduct its own survey, followed by exploratory drilling in promising places with 2.2-million-pound mobile drill rigs. And that's just to look for oil. Never mind extracting and transporting it.

Ronnie Chappell, BP Alaska's affable director of press and publications, took our by now somewhat shabby crew on an excruciatingly thorough tour of Endicott, BP's state-of-the-art production facility on the outskirts of Prudhoe Bay. Ken Boyd, the former director of the Alaska State Division of Oil and Gas, was working with Ronnie on the tour. As a helpful fellow in overalls explained the minutiae of directional drilling, I chatted with Ken: Why is Alaska so intent on opening the refuge? After all, there are abundant opportunities to the west that the oil industry is already pursuing, and the 1002 makes up a fraction—only 4 percent—of Alaska's coastal plain.

"Oil is what Alaska has," Ken said. "If the state had other options, we'd try them. I believe we can drill in the ANWR without causing any damage, and I think we have to do it."

"Is there any place in the state you'd consider off-limits, any place you'd hate to see drilled?"

"If it could be done in an environmentally sensitive way, no."

A growing number of our nation's scientists are determining that drilling in the Arctic Refuge cannot be done in an environmentally sensitive way. The American Society of Mammalogists recently passed a resolution recommending that no drilling take place in the refuge. Audubon Alaska coordinated an open letter from 500 scientists, including George Schaller and E.O. Wilson, urging President Bush to reconsider his position in the face of "five decades of biological study and scientific research." They asked that he "permanently protect the biological diversity and wilderness character of the coastal plain of the Arctic National Wildlife Refuge from future oil and gas development."

And a growing body of evidence suggests that environmentally sensitive drilling may in fact be the contradiction in terms it sounds like. Twice now, the *Wall Street Journal*, no hotbed of environmental activism, has run articles expressing concern that "oil-rig technology touted by President Bush as environmentally friendly and central to his expanded drilling plans has malfunctioned at rising rates in the past five years on rigs in western Prudhoe Bay."

To this writer, the issue of whether or not the coastal plain can be drilled carefully—made into a sort of Prudhoe Lite—seems beside the point. With the placement of a single length of pipeline in the wilderness we will have stepped over a threshold from which there is no turning back. We will have transformed our "symbolic landscape" into something else: an industrial site. Then we will have to look elsewhere for wilderness.

At the Fish and Wildlife Service office in Fairbanks I saw a picture I'll remember. It showed a shallow rut, straight as a plumb line, running away across the tundra. It is one of 200 sites that botanists are monitoring, relics of a seismic survey conducted in the dead of winter in 1984. The rut, now a venerable 17 years old, shows where a seismic truck compacted soil and scuffed away vegetation. The tundra has still not recovered.

There is no evidence the scar hurts wildlife. After all, it's just a rut. And yet it might as well be a chasm, an impossibly straight, lettuce-green abyss that cuts directly to the heart of the debate: Does the fact that there might be oil in the refuge justify industrializing this rare and precious place? Or, regardless of what's under it, shall we make the Arctic Refuge one of the few American places we keep entirely wild?

8

Oil Drilling Should Be Allowed in the Arctic National Wildlife Refuge

Paul Weyrich

Paul Weyrich is chairman and CEO of the Free Congress Foundation, a politically and culturally conservative think tank.

The American economy thrives on cheap oil. As demand for this precious resource grows, the United States should drill in every region where petroleum is available. Modern oil extraction methods are friendlier to the environment than those used in past decades. The ANWR wilderness should be managed for the greatest good to the most people. To lock up this large reserve of oil with wilderness protection regulations would be irresponsible to energy users in decades to come.

America's greens chalked up a 'victory' when the United States Senate voted [in March 2003] to keep funding for oil drilling in the Arctic National Wildlife Refuge out of the fiscal year 2004 budget.

Not surprisingly, the Sierra Club's national office trumpeted the vote as one "to protect this spectacular (Alaskan) landscape." And it also makes the claim with a straight face to be for reducing our dependence on foreign oil.

We both agree on the last point. But the Sierra Club sees your SUV and its thirst for gas as the problem in our achieving that important goal; this powerful green lobby pushes for developing unproven technologies such as wind power and solar energy as the answer to our energy problems.

Most conservatives—count me among them—and many scientists do not see the answer to our energy problems to be blowing in the wind. But we do see the Sierra Club and like-minded green lobbies to be a big part of the problem in lessening our reliance on foreign oil. They are standing in the way of developing ANWR and other key projects that could yield more energy for our nation.

By opposing development of ANWR, the Sierra Club is preventing us from taking a practical step to increase our nation's energy security.

Paul Weyrich, "ANWR: Untapped Resource in Fight for Energy Independence," www.newsmax.com, March 28, 2003. Copyright © 2003 by Newsmax.com. Reproduced by permission of author.

Environmental lobbies like to scare people away from developing ANWR by showing pretty pictures of Alaska's towering mountains and green valleys and beautiful lakes and its wildlife, implying that they will all be ruined if exploration and development of ANWR is allowed to proceed.

Secretary Norton and others in the Bush administration vow that . . . they will keep pushing until the green light is given for exploration and drilling. Good!

Yet, as Secretary of the Interior Gate Norton told the U.S. House Committee on Resources, the specific area of ANWR where exploration for oil would take place has "no trees, there are no deepwater lakes. There are no mountains." The polar bears and musk oxen and caribou have done well in those places in Alaska where oil development is already taking place.

A great prospect for future oil

The real story about ANWR is very different from what is featured in the propaganda of environmental groups.

The ANWR proposal, if passed by Congress and signed into law, would include stringent environmental protection. But Secretary Norton asks this question: "As we consider the environmental factors affecting the congressional choice about ANWR, one might ask what environmental protections are used in other countries on which we rely for 57 percent of our oil?"

More importantly, the U.S. Department of Energy estimates that ANWR could yield as much 1,369,863 barrels of oil daily. Texas produces 1,065,753 barrels, followed by Alaska (non-ANWR) with 972,603 barrels.

Norton recently told the Committee on Resources that the United States Geological Survey estimates that ANWR has an estimated 10.4 billion barrels of technically recoverable oil. She said, "The potential daily production from [ANWR] is larger than the current daily onshore oil production of any of the lower 48 [states]." She calls ANWR our "nation's single greatest onshore prospect for future oil."

It will take years to develop ANWR, something that Norton admitted when she noted that Americans "have now heard for more than 15 years that [ANWR] isn't worth developing on the Coastal Plain because it would take ten years to get the oil to market. If we had begun exploration and development when the Congress first proposed it," then some of ANWR's oil would be in a pipeline heading toward the Lower 48 today.

There are very good reasons why we should move as a nation toward energy independence based on concerns of economic and national security, namely protecting our country from threats of blackmail or revenge from oil-rich foreign countries and holding the line on our balance of trade.

Secretary Norton and others in the Bush administration vow that we have not heard the last of ANWR, that they will keep pushing until the green light is given for exploration and drilling. Good! We need energy at a time when our own supplies are at risk because of the volatile political climates in the Middle East and South America.

We do not have oil from ANWR now and will not in the future if the Sierra Club and other groups continue to thwart allowing exploration and development of it there.

If we are to have an effective, workable program for reducing our dependence on foreign oil, then ANWR has to be a very important part of it. The Sierra Club and other environmental groups have spent 15 years lobbying to stop development of ANWR, succeeding so far through their use of scare tactics.

The obstructionism of the green lobby should not be allowed to continue at this critical time for our nation. Congress needs to give the go-ahead to explore and develop what stands to become our nation's most important source of oil here at home.

9

The Forest Service Should Improve Its Management of the Tongass National Forest

Southeast Alaska Conservation Council

The Southeast Alaska Conservation Council (SEACC) is a coalition of volunteer conservation groups in Alaskan communities surrounded by the Tongass National Forest. These groups want to safeguard the Tongass's world-class environment while providing for the sustainable use of the region's resources.

The National Forest Service loses hundreds of millions of dollars every year on timber sales in America's wilderness. The government spends money in order to manage sales, survey land, and builds roads. Meanwhile, timber companies pay only a small percentage of what the lumber is worth. This problem is clearly seen in the Tongass National Forest, which contains 9.3 million acres of timber. Tongass is the world's largest, intact temperate rain forest, and its wild forests and waters are home to bears, eagles, salmon, whales, and other endangered species. Incredibly, taxpayers subsidize logging companies to destroy this phenomenal wilderness as a few large corporations clear-cut thousands of acres of publicly owned, old-growth timber that has a minimal value on the open market. Although proponents claim that logging creates much-needed jobs, most of the timber is sold intact to manufacturing and processing plants outside of Alaska. This inexplicably destructive management of one of the planet's most beautiful wilderness areas benefits only a few well-connected corporations.

Since 1982, American taxpayers have spent almost one billion dollars supporting activities related to logging on the Tongass. The U.S. Forest Service has consistently lost more taxpayer money on the Tongass timber program than any other National Forest.

In 2002, the Forest Service spent more than $36 million of U.S. taxpayer money preparing timber sales and building logging roads on the

Tongass. Yet, private timber companies paid the federal government just $1.2 million in return for the right to cut down about a thousand acres of old-growth forest, resulting in a nearly $35 million subsidy to the timber industry. These taxpayer subsidies directly benefit private timber companies that are logging at the expense of other forest users.

The Forest Service estimates that it spends more than $100 of taxpayer money to prepare, administer, and support every thousand board feet of Tongass timber it sells. Yet the agency estimates a return on this expense of only $36 per thousand board feet.

U.S. taxpayers spent more than $178,000 for every direct timber job created by logging on the Tongass National Forest in 2002.

Massive taxpayer looses on the Tongass helped fuel passage of the Tongass Timber Reform Act in 1990. The law repealed a mandatory $40 million annual appropriation for road building and logging on the Tongass put in place in 1980.

But the losses have not stopped. According to a 1995 General Accounting Office [GAO] report, the Tongass timber program cost American taxpayers more than $102 million between 1992 and 1994. The timber program lost another $69 million between 1995 and 1997. . . .

Building roads to nowhere

Taxpayers spend millions of appropriated dollars every year designing and laying out "roads to nowhere" throughout the Tongass. In 2002, the Forest Service spent millions of appropriated dollars building roads that to nowhere except to stands of publicly owned old-growth rainforest. Private timber companies then use these roads to haul away public timber for their own profit.

The Tongass already has a 5,000 mile road system, enough roads to drive from Seattle to Miami and then north to Boston. Because of the Tongass' many islands, only 800 miles of the existing logging road system are accessible by ferry or communities, the rest are largely abandoned logging roads.

Despite the high cost, the Forest Service shows no sign of slowing its road building. Although the Forest Service states "roads pose the greatest risk to fish resources on the Tongass," it still plans to build another 1,065 miles of new logging roads over the next decade, enough roads to drive from Boston to St. Louis. Over the next fifty years, it plans to build 2,800 more miles of roads, increasing the miles of existing roads by more than 50 percent.

U.S. taxpayers spent more than $178,000 for every direct timber job created by logging on the Tongass National Forest in 2002.

While it continues to build new roads, the Forest Service is unable to maintain its existing logging road system. The agency has an estimated road maintenance backlog in Southeast Alaska of nearly $100 million. For example, the Forest Service and Alaska Department of Fish and Game

(ADF&G) have identified more than 1,500 stream culverts (the metal pipes under roads) that fall to meet standards for allowing salmon and other fish to swim under the logging roads. The problems should be fixed before the Forest Service builds expensive new roads into pristine and controversial areas of the Tongass.

Because of its high costs, questionable returns, and environmental impacts, the building of new logging roads into pristine areas is highly controversial at both the national and local levels.

Noncompetitive bidding

The majority of timber sales the Forest Service sells on the Tongass National Forest only have one bidder. Without bidding competition, timber companies have no reason to pay above a minimum rate, far below actual timber sale preparation costs. Taxpayers end up paying the difference.

The Forest Service also spends millions of dollars preparing timber sales that no one buys. Between 1998 and 2001, the Forest Service failed to sell 30 percent of the timber sales it spent tax dollars to prepare and offer.

The timber industry and its political supporters are now pressuring the Forest Service to create special long-term timber contracts that would allow timber companies to hang on to standing timber for up to 10 years until the "price is right" to cut. Time will tell whether these special contracts will enhance competition among the industry players that potentially could result in reduced taxpayer subsidies. If past experience with long-term contracts is any indication, taxpayers shouldn't count on obtaining relief. During the era of the two fifty-year monopoly pulp timber contracts that ruled the Tongass from 1954 until 1997, taxpayers paid hundreds of millions in subsidies so that the multi-national timber companies could buy Tongass rainforest trees at non-competitive, bargain-basement prices.

Unfortunately for the timber industry, the bill for years of unsustainable logging has come due. The stands of timber standing on the Tongass today are less economical, less accessible, and more important to other resource users like recreation businesses, communities, hunters, and fishermen than they were 50 years ago.

Today, more than 70 percent of the biggest and best timber stands that once stood in Southeast Alaska are gone. Remaining pockets of old-growth rainforest protect streams full of wild salmon, provide deer for hunters, and are important for tourism, recreation, and Native Alaskans and other Alaskans who live a subsistence lifestyle.

While the Tongass is the nation's largest national forest, the vast majority of this landscape is rock, ice, and scrub timber. Although there are 5.5 million acres of what the Forest Service terms "productive forest land" on the Tongass, the vast majority of these lands will never be economical to log. In contrast, the acres the Forest Service plans to clearcut are the biological and economic heart of the Tongass. Many users depend on the same rare, large, high-value trees that the Forest Service targets for logging.

The timber industry blames environmental laws and the environmental groups that support them for high taxpayer losses on the Tongass. However, the facts do not support its criticism. The Tongass timber program has been a consistent money loser during the last twenty years.

There is no relationship between the amount of the subsidies and changes in environmental law or policy.

Environmental reviews of timber sales under the National Environmental Policy Act (NEPA) are important because they identify and document the harmful effects that logging projects have on salmon, bear, deer, and other fish and wildlife habitat. Additionally, they provide local citizens and other Americans opportunities to comment on proposed sales. The cost to the Forest Service to do these critical environmental reviews is nearly one and a half times less that the cost for timber sale preparation, administration, and engineering support.

Today, more than 70 percent of the biggest and best timber stands that once stood in Southeast Alaska are gone.

Efforts to hold the Forest Service accountable for compliance with federal and state laws are also not to blame. Of the $414 million the Forest Service spent on the Tongass timber program (including road maintenance) from 1991 through 2002, only $1.6 million—*less than one-half of one percent*—was spent on appeals and litigation.

Logging on lands owned by the State of Alaska, that receive far less environmental protection and oversight than the Tongass National Forest, also loses money. In fiscal year 2002, the State of Alaska spent $9,900,200 on its timber program. These sales returned just $446,700.

Timber jobs decline despite huge subsidies

Justified on the basis of providing jobs, the Tongass timber program continues to provide fewer and fewer employment opportunities for Southeast Alaskans. Despite large taxpayer subsidies, the Tongass timber industry has continued to lose jobs in the face of tough world competition, unforgiving world timber markets, and fundamental timber market changes.

Despite its persistent claims to the contrary, the Tongass timber industry continues to be flush with both timber and taxpayer cash.

At the end of July 2003, the timber industry had nearly 300 million board feet of timber (mmbf) under contract or available, free and clear of litigation, that could be cut at any time. This amounts to a 6-year supply of timber at the 10-year average annual independent logging level and over a 4-year supply at the 20-year level. To put things in perspective, one million board feet of timber would cover one acre, two feet deep, or provide enough lumber to build 120 houses.

Demand for Tongass timber in world markets has dropped sharply. In recent years, many Tongass timber sales have gone unsold or uncut. However, the Forest Service continues to spend millions of dollars laying out new sales, often in controversial areas.

The most reliable customer in the past for Tongass wood products—Japan—is wrestling with economic stagnation and is substituting higher quality wood products and inexpensive Russian logs for the Alaskan wood products it once purchased. These changes likely are permanent and "not simply the down side of a cycle. . . . Aggressive new competitors, with new and often superior products, permanently established themselves [in the Japanese market] and began expanding their market shares."

In 2000, North American log exports to Japan declined by 37 percent from 1994 levels; total log and lumber exports declined by 38 percent during the same period. In 2001, total Japanese log and lumber imports from North America reached the lowest level since 1965. As noted in a December 2001–January 2002 Pacific Rim Wood Market Report:

> A special challenge, with long-term implications, is the weakened market for hemlock lumber in Japan. . . . It has traditionally found a ready market in Japan, where it is sold green. . . . [However,] new building codes (following the Kobe earthquake in 1995) have resulted in green hemlock losing favor to kiln-dried lumber readily available from Scandinavia and elsewhere.

In May 2003, the Alaska Department of Labor predicted a continued decline in timber jobs: "low prices for milled timber, . . . a national glut of timber, and sharp Canadian competition all point to continuing erosion in the logging and wood products industries."

Markets and the pulp mills

By 1997, Alaska's two pulp mills had closed their doors, even though both had significant timber supplies at their disposal. In fact, the Ketchikan Pulp Company continued to log Tongass timber already approved for its use for three years after it shut down its pulp mill.

Several factors contributed to these mill closures, including worldwide competition, high worldwide pulp inventories, and declining pulp prices. The competition came from newer, larger, and more efficient pulp mills in South Africa, Brazil, and elsewhere. In a quarterly report filed with the Securities and Exchange Commission, Louisiana-Pacific Corporation stated: "large worldwide pulp inventories at the end of 1995 have carried through the first six months of 1996, creating very weak pulp markets.". . .

The Forest Service says that worldwide markets for Alaskan wood products are now so low that 90–95 percent of all existing timber contracts are unprofitable. In fact, in late 2002, the Forest Service gave timber contract holders a 3-year extension to allow them to hold on to the timber they had already purchased rather than cut it at a loss.

In justifying this extension, the Chief of the Forest Service said "the lumber market in 2001 was at its lowest level in 10 years. Purchasers of National Forest System timber in Alaska are unable to harvest the timber sales without incurring losses that threaten bankruptcy, mill closures, or severe economic losses."

The Tongass timber industry is a high-cost producer in a competitive world market. Relative to British Columbia, the Pacific Northwest, and other competitors, the Tongass has higher labor and production costs, higher vulnerability to relatively small price fluctuations in world hemlock prices, and a higher likelihood of being out-competed by engineered wood products.

One result of these global economic changes is a large number of unsold timber sales on the Tongass. Between 1998 and 2001, more than 30 percent of Tongass timber sales failed to attract even a single bidder. As a result, millions of taxpayer dollars the Forest Service spent laying out these sales have been largely wasted.

While timber markets have permanently and radically changed, the Forest Service continues to ask for and receive more money to produce more timber sales as if nothing has changed.

Fiscal year 2002 saw one of the lowest logging levels on record—just 34 million board feet—the lowest level since 1940. Yet, the Forest Service continues to use a flawed economic model to argue that market demand for timber on the Tongass is 152 million board feet, a logging level reached by independent loggers just twice in the last twenty years.

The Forest Service's estimate of market demand is important because the Forest Service uses this estimate to justify its annual request to Congress for funding. The higher the estimate of market demand, the more money the Forest Service gets for timber sales on the Tongass, even if the estimate flies in the face of reality.

Trying to meet the Forest Service's unrealistic estimate of market demand for timber costs tens of millions of taxpayer dollars a year. It also forces the Forest Service to lay out timber sales and build roads in highly controversial areas. These include roadless areas that are important to many other users of the Tongass.

Nevertheless, the timber industry and its political supporters want the Forest Service to provide 360 million board feet of timber a year. This amount is more than twice the Forest Service's estimate of market demand and nearly five times the 20-year average annual cut. The Forest Service has determined this logging level to be unsustainable over time. Not only would it significantly impact other users of the Tongass, but, if logging the Tongass continues losing money at the rate it has since 1982, *it would cost taxpayers more than $50 million each year* to log this much timber.

Taxpayer subsidies on the Tongass largely benefit a declining industry that provides few jobs and economic benefits compared to other sectors of the region's economy.

Too many trees clearcut on the Tongass are shipped as unprocessed round logs to Asia and the Pacific Northwest without producing any manufacturing or wood processing jobs in Alaska. In fact, the Forest Service allowed timber companies to export a volume equal to 23 percent of the total timber logged on the Tongass in 2000 and 2001 as raw logs with no processing or manufacturing in Alaska.

Logs were also exported without Alaska processing from state-owned lands, University of Alaska lands, Mental Health Trust lands, and private lands. Between 1990 and 2002, more than 6.1 billion board feet of timber, worth $3.6 billion has been exported from Alaska as raw unmanufactured logs without creating a single processing or manufacturing job in the state.

While exports of Tongass trees include all species of commercially important conifers, most of the trees exported are cedars. Alaska yellow cedar is highly regarded for specialty products and brings high returns to timber companies. Almost all of the yellow cedar cut on the Tongass is exported directly to Asia as round logs. Most western red cedar cut on the Tongass is also exported as raw unmanufactured logs. . . .

A fully developed, high value-added industry could support 14–18 jobs per million board feet of timber utilized. Forest Service data show that for the years 1997 through 2001, the average annual volume of trees exported was approximately 30 mmbf. If this timber had been manufactured into value-added products in Alaska, it could have supported approximately 480 additional jobs a year for Alaskans.

Unfortunately, today Tongass trees, Alaskan jobs, and U.S. tax dollars continue to be exported at unreasonably high levels.

Future investments: where should they go?

Is Southeast Alaska getting the biggest bang for the taxpayer buck? Given the huge subsidies federal taxpayers are sending to Southeast Alaska, is the region making the best of these public investments? Are the subsidies supporting jobs and an investment in the region's long-term future, or are they an expensive attempt to hold on to a post that no longer exists?

Today, taxpayer subsidies on the Tongass largely benefit a declining industry that provides few jobs and economic benefits compared to other sectors of the region's economy. These subsidies also fund activities that are controversial in the region and across the country because they degrade one of the world's rarest and most valued landscapes.

These subsidies could provide more jobs and do less environmental damage if they were invested in smarter ways. Tourism, recreation, and environmental restoration are a few of the many examples for how these funds could be better invested. Other possibilities include the marketing of Alaskan salmon and high value-added wood products.

While the timber industry is declining and providing increasingly fewer jobs in Southeast Alaska, tourism and recreation continue to grow.

Cruise ships alone brought an estimated 632,000 visitors to Southeast Alaska in 2000, compared to 235,000 visitors in 1990. The number of clients using outfitters and guides has also climbed sharply during the last decade. Outfitter/guide clients increased from approximately 1,550 in 1994 to 14,000 in 1999, an increase of 800 percent in five years.

The growth of recreation and tourism is a national trend. According to the Forest Service's 2000 Strategic Plan, by far the largest economic activity in the National Forest System is recreation use,[1] followed by hunting, fishing, and wildlife viewing. Timber holds a distant 3rd place.

This Plan also shows that, in 1999, recreation use in National Forests represented 64 percent of the total dollar amount of National Forest resource outputs.[2] The category of hunting, fishing, and wildlife viewing represented another 16 percent of those outputs. Together these two recreational categories made up 80 percent of all national forest resource

---

1. In the Strategic Plan, "recreation use" includes all recreation activities except hunting, fishing, and wildlife viewing.   2. "Output" is defined as "measurable goods, end products, or services resulting from management activities that are purchased, consumed, or used directly by people."

outputs when measured in terms of their dollar values. In contrast, timber was responsible for just 11 percent. Mineral and energy extraction equaled 7 percent.

In terms of employment, the Plan showed that the impact of recreation was greater still. The two recreational categories made up 85 percent of jobs produced; the two resource extraction categories just 13 percent.

A 1997 comparison between the value of logging Tongass old-growth forest and recreation and tourism use of these lands showed the latter was nine times more valuable than logging. By 2000, recreation and tourism on the Tongass contributed 30 times the value of clearcutting the forest. Clearly, trees left standing for recreation and tourism contribute substantially more than logging to Southeast Alaska's long-term economy.

Recreation, tourism, and commercial fishing related to the Tongass provide far more jobs and income to the region's economy than the timber industry. In 2001, 51 percent of resource-dependent Southeast Alaska jobs were in recreation and tourism and 9 percent were in wood products. When the Tongass region's salmon harvesting and seafood processing are added in, 87 percent of Southeast Alaska resource-based employment, and 19 percent of all Southeast Alaska employment, was due to recreation, tourism, and commercial fishing.

Salmon harvesting and seafood processing produced more than 3,000 jobs in 2001. Recreation and tourism accounted for 4,278 jobs in Southeast Alaska, more than 5 times the number of jobs in the timber industry. Most of the tourism and recreation jobs were associated with small businesses. The Alaska Division of Community and Business Development identified 736 commercial recreation businesses working in the Tongass region in 2000, and the number is probably higher.

The Forest Service has unique opportunities to invest in projects that will employ hard-working Alaskans doing skilled work to restore the environment and protect natural resources.

Most timber jobs in the region are associated with private lands. The Forest Service estimates that the Tongass National Forest provided 195 timber jobs in 2002, less than 0.6 percent of the total jobs in the region's economy.

Timber, recreation, and tourism jobs are *all* important. But the trend is clear: jobs in the timber industry are declining while jobs in the recreation and tourism sector are increasing.

While the Forest Service prides itself on being a multiple-use agency, it's not a multiple-use subsidizer. Tourism, recreation, and commercial fishing provide far more jobs and economic benefits to the region than the timber industry, but they are clearly lower Forest Service funding priorities.

The agency consistently spends two and a half times more money on Tongass logging and logging roads than it does on tourism and recreation. Similarly, it spends four times more each year on logging and road building than it does on fish and wildlife management activities.

The Forest Service has starved its recreation program over the last decade. While the need to plan and manage tourism and recreation growth has grown dramatically on the Tongass, the agency's recreation budget has stagnated. In fact, while the number of clients using outfitter/guide services increased by 800 percent from 1994 to 1999, the Forest Service's budget allocation for recreation, wilderness, and heritage management on the Tongass actually dropped 20 percent during the same time period. The agency needs to invest now in planning and managing the ever-increasing levels of tourism and recreational use on the Tongass in order to avoid conflicts among commercial users and non-commercial users, including local residents, and to safeguard the natural resources that provide for the "wild Alaska" experience. . . .

If the Forest Service really cared about jobs in the Tongass region, it would get a bigger bang for the taxpayer buck by investing less in logging and more in other sectors of the region's economy.

A healthy environment generates jobs and earnings

Wildlife viewing, recreational (sport) hunting and fishing, and subsistence activities on the Tongass also generate millions of dollars every year. Data on numbers of participants and the economic value of their spending have been consistently difficult to obtain for the Tongass; nevertheless, the studies that have been done illustrate the popularity of activities that depend upon maintaining healthy ecosystems on the forest.

[One study] showed that in 1993, anglers spent about $103 million ($49 million by residents, $54 million by visitors) for sport fishing in Southeast Alaska. This spending directly supported an estimated 1,260 jobs with a payroll worth an estimated $27 million. Conducting most of their hunts on Tongass land, sport hunters spent $6 million on deer, moose, and mountain goat hunting in 1984 and 1985, an expenditure equal to $9.2 million today. Bear hunting also draws hundreds of residents and visitors to the Tongass. Brown bear hunts on Admiralty, Baranof, and Chichagof islands are a particularly lucrative activity; non-Alaskan hunters are required to be accompanied by a guide, who typically charges $10,000 per hunt. The 93 brown bears taken by non-residents from these islands in 1998 represent nearly $1 million in guiding fees alone.

Wildlife viewing is immensely popular on the Tongass. The Forest Service's National Visitor Use Monitoring program identified wildlife viewing as the most popular activity of visitors to the Tongass in 2000. Indeed, visitors to Southeast Alaska expect to view wildlife and are willing to pay for that experience. In the summer of 1989, viewers spent an estimated $43.1 million to see wildlife. A survey sponsored by the ADF&G and the Forest Service found that the more a person was motivated to take a trip to Alaska to view wildlife, the more money they were likely to spend in the state during their trip, the longer they were likely to stay, and the greater the chance that they would visit more than one region of the state. . . .

Healthy ecosystems, beautiful scenery, and the fish and wildlife they produce generate millions of dollars a year for Southeast Alaskans and help sustain the region economically.

The Forest Service has unique opportunities to invest in projects that will employ hard-working Alaskans doing skilled work to restore the environment and protect natural resources important to the region's economy.

The Tongass has huge environmental restoration needs. The Forest Service and ADF&G have identified more than 1,500 stream culverts that do not pass the Forest Service standards for allowing fish to swim through. The culverts are too steep or the end of the pipe is hanging too far above the water for fish to move up and down streams to reach critical habitat. To protect Alaska's rich salmon and trout fisheries, these culverts need to be replaced or repaired as soon as possible. . . .

There are also other problems with the 5,000 miles of logging roads already criss-crossing the Tongass. The Forest Service can't afford to maintain them and most are virtually abandoned. These unmaintained roads increase the likelihood of erosion, sedimentation, and landslides, harming fish habitat.

The Forest Service has a road maintenance backlog in Alaska totaling nearly $100 million. The backlog grows every year. The annual maintenance needs for the road system on the Tongass National Forest is $17.6 million alone. But in 2002, the Forest Service spent only $3.5 million on road maintenance, *From 1993–2000, the average annual road maintenance budget was only $1.7 million, less than 10 percent of the annual need.* At the same time, the Forest Service continues to spend millions of dollars a year building new logging roads, most of them serving no public purpose.

If the Tongass timber program is a "jobs program", the Forest Service should invest in repairing its existing logging roads, before it continues to build new logging roads at great taxpayer expense and environmental damage. . . .

Investing in the future, not the past

Southeast Alaska's economic landscape has changed dramatically over the last decade, and it will likely continue changing in the future. If the Forest Service is interested in helping provide jobs in Southeast Alaska, it must begin to invest more in the future. . . .

The Forest Service could generate more jobs and income in Southeast Alaska if it invested more in tourism, recreation, restoration, and smaller scale, value-added manufacturing. The Forest Service could invest in expanding its visitor facilities, building and maintaining campgrounds, building and maintaining Tongass trails, replacing culverts that block fish passage, and planning for tourism and recreation growth. These investments would benefit local Southeast Alaskans as well as the hundreds of thousands of Americans who visit the famed Inside Passage every year.

Small-scale, value-added wood products manufacturing, government, and commercial fishing will also continue to play key roles in Southeast Alaska's economy, as will other economic sectors that share what is special and unique about Alaska in a way that is competitive with world markets.

This is not to suggest that tourism, recreation, restoration, and value-added manufacturing should be the only areas in which the Forest Service invests. Indeed, tourism and recreation, for example, bring their own impacts to communities and the environment, impacts that citizens of the Tongass will have to work together to balance.

10

Logging the Tongass National Forest Can Provide Many Benefits

U.S. Forest Service

The U.S. Forest Service manages the nation's forests, including the Tongass National Forest in southeast Alaska.

The U.S. Forest Service permits logging in the Tongass National Forest because of the numerous benefits it provides. First, culling old-growth trees improves forest health and reduces the risk of catastrophic fire. Second, clearings made by loggers provide vital grazing areas for deer and other wildlife. Finally, allowing logging in the forest provides jobs to Alaskan residents and pumps money into the local economy.

Haven't 70% of the biggest trees and best timber stands [in the Tongass National Forest] already been logged?

About seven percent of the total productive old-growth (400,000 acres out of 5,400,000 acres) has been harvested over the last 100 years. About 15% of the very highest high volume stands have been harvested, while about 85% of the Forest's highest volume old-growth remains unharvested. Over the next 100 years, the Forest Plan permits harvest of less than ten percent more of the high volume old-growth.

Isn't the part of the Tongass National Forest where logging isn't allowed all rocks, ice and muskeg?

There are about 5 million acres of "commercial-size" timber stands on the Tongass; of which about 4.5 million acres, or 90%, are off-limits to timber harvesting. Over the next 100 years, the current Forest Plan will permit harvest of an additional 3–4% of the productive old-growth reducing it from about 90% to around 87%. An additional 4.2 million acres of low-productivity forest also will not have timber harvesting activities.

Won't the timber harvests scheduled by the Forest Service "rip the biological heart" out of the Tongass?

The Forest Plan was designed and written specifically to protect the

U.S. Forest Service, "Questions and Answers: Tongass National Forest," www.fs.fed.us, February 12, 2004.

"biological heart" of the Forest. The Tongass National Forest Plan has been scientifically reviewed by independent biologists who found it to be fully capable of meeting our obligations to manage habitat to maintain well-distributed, viable wildlife populations. The old-growth strategy is designed to provide for a level of timber harvest that is consistent with protecting other resource values.

Isn't logging harmful to fish and wildlife habitat?

Forest management can be consistent with wildlife objectives. There are especially bright prospects for partial cutting on the Tongass. Managing for a mosaic of forest patches has been suggested for deer in Southeast Alaska. In addition, recent work suggests that certain types of partial cutting conserves deer habitat and old-growth structure, while maintaining the health of the forest. Silvicultural treatment in second growth stands also enhances habitat for deer and other species that depend on undergrowth. . . .

[The logging plan is] fully capable of meeting our obligations to manage habitat to maintain well-distributed, viable wildlife populations.

Why does the Forest Service keep selling timber, when there isn't any real demand for the wood?

The economy of Southeast Alaska consists of tourism, fishing, service industries, recreation, mining and timber. The timber industry is an important leg that supports the larger economy of the State and Southeast Alaska. The Tongass National Forest Plan recognized the need to preserve the biological heart of the forest while providing for the inclusion of jobs on the human-side of the ecosystem equation. Timber harvest is scheduled over the next 100 years on approximately 4% of the land-base. Timbering and providing pristine wild country to future generations of Americans can and do co-exist on the Tongass National Forest in Southeast Alaska.

The timber industry is in a transition period since the pulp mill contracts have been terminated and timber producers are finding new markets for the lower grade logs. Mill operators from the lower 48 are interested in opening new manufacturing facilities in Southeast Alaska which by itself speaks to market demand. The Wood Testing Research Center in Ketchikan is concluding tests that positively display that wood from the Tongass has high qualities including breaking and stiffness strengths greater than that of Douglas-fir. The industry is currently applying for wood grades from the American Lumber Standards Committee for Alaska yellow cedar, western hemlock and Sitka spruce. Demand is expected to increase as the standards are approved and implemented. The largest unknown for the timber industry is environmental appeal and litigation of the environmental analysis completed for future timber sales.

The Forest Service versus the timber industry

Isn't the Forest Service subsidizing the timber industry in Southeast Alaska by losing $35 million . . . a year on the Tongass?

The cost of compliance with various federal planning requirements including the National Environmental Policy Act (NEPA) plus the costs of responding to NEPA appeals and litigation costs approximately $110 per thousand board feet.

The cost of timber sale field preparation, appraisal, advertisement and field sale administration costs approximately $36 per thousand board feet. The stumpage for the Forest Service volume under contract averages $41 per thousand board feet.

For a variety of reasons, profitability is a poor yardstick for evaluating the performance of the national forest timber sale program:

• *The national forests are not managed like a private timber growing business.*—As a matter of law and policy, the national forest timber program is not managed like a private timber growing business. Important differences revolve around such things as the longer growing periods (i.e., rotations) and higher stocking levels that are commonly employed, the greater emphasis placed on natural and uneven-aged management as opposed to plantation and even-aged management, the greater emphasis placed on the non-timber benefits obtainable from forest lands, the greater emphasis placed on thoroughly analyzing all the potential environmental effects of proposed timber sale projects, and the more open administrative processes and procedures that are employed—e.g., the agency's administrative appeals process. If we do not want national forest managers to behave like private forest managers, does it make sense to judge their performance by the private sector's main performance standard—i.e., profits?

• *Timber sales are oftentimes the "least net cost" method of achieving desired management objectives.*—As noted earlier, timber sales are increasingly being used mainly as a tool for achieving various land management objectives, other than fiber production, that require manipulating the existing vegetation—e.g., improving forest health and reducing the risk of catastrophic fire. While sales of this type are frequently below-cost, the net cost to the government of achieving such land stewardship goals is oftentimes minimized when a timber sale is used to attain the desired ends. This result is explained by the fact that timber sales, unlike the other ways of manipulating vegetation—e.g., prescribed burning, use of chemical herbicides, and mechanical treatments such as cut-&-leave—typically generate revenue to help offset their implementation costs.

The . . . Plan recognized the need to preserve the biological heart of the forest while providing for the inclusion of jobs.

• *Timber sales provide many benefits beyond the revenues earned.*—Returns to the US Treasury are only one of the benefits derived from national forest timber sales. From an economic standpoint there are the job opportunities that are created, the additional income that accrues to individuals and businesses, the increment in tax receipts that governments receive by virtue of taxing this added income, the improved forest access that occurs as a result of timber-related road construction and reconstruction activities, and the legally required receipt-share payments that go to benefit local schools and roads. From an ecologic standpoint, there are the various land stewardship objectives that are addressed through timber harvesting—e.g., the improvements in forest health, the reductions in the risk of catastrophic fire, and the enhanced habitat conditions for wildlife. As the economic account . . . has consistently shown, to the extent that we can quantify them, the present value of the long-term benefits associated with national forest timber sales exceed the present value of the long-term costs.

• *There is no legal direction to earn a profit from the sale of national forest timber.*—The statutes under which the national forests are managed do not mandate that the agency make a profit from the sale of timber; indeed, some key laws—e.g., the Multiple Use-Sustained Yield Act of 1960, and the National Forest Management Act of 1976—contain language which explicitly suggests or states that some management decisions should not be based on profit maximization considerations. However, the Forest Service does have an obligation to use taxpayer dollars as efficiently as possible. Even though the national forest timber sale program operates at a financial "loss", this loss does not represent a subsidy of federal timber purchasers.

Tourism

Doesn't logging always harm tourism and subsistence opportunities?

Properly designed timber sales can be either neutral or actually beneficial to both recreation and subsistence users. For example, road-based recreation opportunities are nearly non-existent in Southeast Alaska, except where logging has first built road systems. On Prince of Wales Island, for example, improving and paving part of this road system has greatly improved transportation amongst rural communities while providing greater opportunities for people to enjoy their national forest through road access. These road systems often provide enhanced access for subsistence users as well.

Isn't the Forest Service giving the "crown jewel" of national forests to "timber barons" or "giant multi-national corporations"?

All the sawmills currently operating in Southeast Alaska are community-based, family owned, small businesses. Not only are these enterprises vital parts of the economic life of Southeast Alaska communities, their owners and workers are an important part of the social fabric of the area.

Isn't the Forest Service wasting money building roads to nowhere?

Southeast Alaska is located in the Alexander Archipelago, and consists of numerous islands. All communities in Southeast Alaska are not connected by roads to the outside world with the exception of Haines and Skagway. The large majority of roads that are located in towns of Southeast Alaska and that connect villages on the same island were originally constructed by the Forest Service for timber sale purposes. Along with basic transportation uses, Forest roads are used by recreationists, subsistence users, outfitters and guides. Some of the roads constructed through Forest Service timber sale contracts provide basic access to these users.

11

Natural Gas Drilling Is Damaging the Powder River Basin

Chris Smith

Chris Smith is a journalist who has contributed to Mother Jones *and other national magazines.*

The Bush administration has embarked on an accelerated program of natural gas extraction in the mountains spanning from New Mexico to Montana, creating conflicts among the gas industry, ranchers, and environmentalists. The Powder River Basin in northern Wyoming is at the center of this industrial activity, known as coalbed methane drilling. Environmentalists, biologists, and researchers see coalbed methane drilling as a disaster for the environment. The extraction method utilizes trillions of gallons of precious water in an arid region and leaves behind polluting salts and minerals that are destroying rivers and lakes located miles from the actual drilling. Despite these facts, the Bureau of Land Management has gone forward with this crash program. Those who want to save this area for use by ranchers, hunters, fishermen, and backpackers are strongly opposed to the industrialization of this unique wilderness.

To get a feel for the layout of a natural gas field, you need to get some distance from it. At ground level, you can't see more than a wellhead, or a string of power lines marching toward the horizon. Seen from the air, however, the full picture begins to emerge: a latticework of service roads, compressors, pipelines, and power lines connecting dozens or hundreds of wells.

This is also the reality of coalbed methane drilling—the natural gas industry's current obsession, and an integral part of the Bush administration's national energy policy. And it looks increasingly likely that it will be the future of the Powder River Basin—an unspoiled expanse of rolling prairie and low hills straddling the Wyoming-Montana border.

"This landscape is going to be changed from an open prairie, high plains landscape to an industrial gas field of unprecedented scale," says Jill Morrison, an organizer with the Wyoming-based Powder River Basin Resource Council. From her home near the 12,500-square-mile Basin's western edge, in the foothills of the Bighorn Mountains, Morrison has watched coalbed methane drilling steadily take hold. And Morrison's dire predictions are based on more than just what she's seen happen already.

"This landscape is going to be changed from an open prairie, high plains landscape to an industrial gas field of unprecedented scale."

From Montana to New Mexico, coalbed methane drilling has spread rapidly through the mountain West. But much of that drilling has been on private or state property. For the past two years, the Bush administration has pressed to open hundreds of thousands of acres of federal land to drilling. The biggest prize in that campaign is the Powder River Basin. Now, according to twin environmental impact statements completed by the Bureau of Land Management (BLM), the Basin is in line for up to 66,000 new wells—more than five wells per square mile. And, along with the wells, BLM officials foresee nearly 25,000 miles of new roads, and 47,000 miles of pipelines, power lines and utility corridors. All told, it will be the biggest natural gas play [project] in the bureau's history.

Shortly after the bureau finalized the plans, a consortium of property owners, ranchers, and environmental groups—Morrison's among them—filed suit in federal court, claiming that the bureau had ignored concerns raised by the public. The suit argues that the BLM plans trample the property rights of local landowners, and fail to protect the Basin's water and air. For the time being, the legal challenge has slowed the rush to drill. But no one knows how long the court-imposed calm will last. With the nation facing a natural gas shortage, the pressure from Washington is only intensifying.

Pressure from the oil industry

In 2002, preliminary versions of the dual impact statements prompted an outcry that reached well beyond the Powder River region. Local groups accused the bureau of downplaying or ignoring many of the project's most serious consequences. The Environmental Protection Agency weighed in, giving the statements an "environmentally unsatisfactory" rating. Newspapers from California to New York published editorials calling for the Bush administration to temper its thirst to drill. The pressure paid off: A moratorium on new drilling was declared, and the bureau went back to the drawing board.

Now, with national attention firmly elsewhere, the bureau has returned with its revised plans, ready to lift the moratorium. According to Morrison and others opposed to the drilling initiative, the new plans hew painfully close to the old ones. While conceding that some small changes for the better have been made, Morrison and others point out that the bureau hasn't changed its industry-friendly recommendation for drilling the maximum number of wells possible. Nor has it suggested workable remedies for—or even fully explored, in some cases—the potentially devastating impacts on the region's water, noise and air quality.

Ultimately, environmentalists say, the bureau's new plans offer the same sort of blank check to the energy industry that the first plans did.

"I think the [bureau] has clearly caved in to the pressure from the oil and gas industry and the Bush administration to drill as many wells as fast as possible with as few environmental safeguards as possible," says Gwen Lachelt, executive director of the Oil and Gas Accountability Project in Durango, Colorado, also home to significant coalbed methane development.

For its part, the bureau concedes that there are few major differences between the draft and final versions of the statements. But BLM officials say there's a good reason for that: the original conclusions were sound, and now they have the data to back those conclusions up.

"As we basically redid the analysis, it didn't really change all that much," says Paul Beels, project manager at the bureau's field office in Buffalo, Wyoming.

The bureau also maintains that its impact studies have been as thorough as possible. "We did a good job, a better job than we did last time," says Dave McIlnay, field manager for the bureau's Miles City, Montana, Office.

Huge quantities of waste water

While BLM officials may be satisfied, critics cite a long list of outstanding issues. Topping that list is the bureau's prescription for handling the huge amounts of waste water that coalbed methane drilling generates. The industry's preferred approach—also the cheapest approach—is to simply pour the water onto the surface. The bureau embraced this approach in its preliminary statements. Critics, though, have pointed to the sheer waste: more than a trillion gallons of water would be pumped out of the arid region's meager aquifer, drawing down the water table and potentially drying up wells throughout the Basin. What more, they claim, most of the water won't be fit for any other use after the drillers get done with it.

Much of the water produced by drilling is so full of mineral salts and heavy metals—each well produces 20 tons of salts per year, according to the Montana Department of Environmental Quality—that it actually poses a threat to the soil, wildlife, and crops.

Much of the water produced by drilling is so full of mineral salts and heavy metals . . . that it actually poses a threat to the soil, wildlife, and crops.

"I'm seeing some damages already from what they're dumping in, and they're wanting to dump in more," says Mark Fix, a Montana rancher, farmer and member of the Northern Plains Resource Council, a local sustainable use group. The salt content in his water has tripled in the last two years, he says. If it rises much higher, it will begin to kill anything he plants.

The bureau's new solution is to store the waste water in thousands of open-air pits, each covering an average of six acres. Far cheaper than reclamation methods proposed by environmentalists, the pits are also almost wholly untested. Bureau planners envision the water slowly filtering harmlessly back into the ground, losing its toxic salts and heavy metals while replenishing the water table. Opponents point out an obvious flaw in the approach. While the water held in the basins may slowly filter into the ground, it will also evaporate rapidly in the dry region—meaning that the mineral salts and other pollutants will become even more concentrated.

The bureau simply doesn't want to spend the time and money to responsibly manage coalbed methane drilling.

Tom Darin, Director of Public Lands and Resources for the Wyoming Outdoor Council, suggests that the bureau is playing a "smoke and mirrors" game. He says that the new plans are likely to have the same impacts as the previous solution, "just delayed over time. And possibly the water quality might be even worse."

Others, meanwhile, worry about what will happen when the wells are plugged. Though the bureau insists that its post-drilling efforts will be adequate, many point out that its clean-up record is spotty at best.

"This play is going to last 10, maybe 20 years," says Steve Jones, the Council's Watershed Protection Program Attorney. "And then the coalbed methane water is gone, the reservoirs are going to dry up and we're going to have these pock-marked, salt-rimmed, empty depressions all over the Powder River Basin."

Over the past year, several environmental groups have suggested alternative methods for handling the waste water, such as having it treated or injecting it deep underground, where it can be filtered as it slowly percolates back into the aquifer. The bureau, by and large, has dismissed these ideas as either unworkable or uneconomical.

"That's just been lip service," Darin says.

Increase in haze and dust

One of the bureau's more obvious failings was its failure to even address air quality concerns. According to John Molenar, vice president of Air Resource Specialists, Inc., an air quality consulting firm, the new statements offer a much fuller disclosure. Unfortunately, he adds, that disclosure makes it clear that drilling will lead to huge increases in haze and dust in the Basin's air. And Molenar says the problem may never be addressed. Noting that the final say on permitting will come from state environmental officials in Montana and Wyoming, Molenar says that the bureau simply punted, secure in the knowledge that it didn't have to make the call.

"They hand-waved on that," he says. "That's what they did. You can argue that it's wrong, but they have the right." And Molenar says the states' records aren't encouraging. "They're going to permit everything they possibly can."

While conceding that the bureau must defer to the states, [Molenar] says federal land managers didn't even try to resist the energy lobby's drill-happy impulses.

"Instead of asserting the authority they unquestionably have to manage development in an environmentally responsible manner, they have essentially thrown up their hands and said 'We'll do what industry wants.'" Opponents of the drilling plans say the evidence of a headlong rush to drill is obvious. A bureau court filing from last year offers a glimpse into its priorities:

"Every month that wells are not drilled on federal lands in the Wyoming Powder River Basin, the United States loses valuable coalbed natural gas through drainage . . . BLM estimates that the royalty value alone of the resource it is losing each month is about $1.4 million."

Even the National Park Service, the bureau's sister agency, has expressed dissatisfaction with the new impact statements. In a scathing letter of protest, the Park Service demanded that the bureau allow more time to study how methane drilling in the Powder River Basin will impact air quality in national treasures like Badlands and Mount Rushmore, which lie downwind.

"Our cursory review of the subject documents indicates that the concerns we raised in our April 12, 2002 comment remain unresolved. We are particularly concerned that the project may result in significant or potentially adverse impacts to several units of the National Park System."

Like many other opponents of the BLM drilling scheme, Morrison says the bureau simply doesn't want to spend the time and money to responsibly manage coalbed methane drilling. Backed by a White House eager to see the wells built, and lured by the promise of billions of dollars in new revenue, the bureau isn't about to let the worrisome reality of coalbed methane stand in its way, she says.

"They're completely sugarcoating it," she says. "We're in a state of denial about this, because [otherwise] we'd really have to deal with the consequences up-front. But what we want is the quick, short-term dollar. We want that money fast, and we're not gonna go in with our eyes open. We're gonna go in telling ourselves a fairy tale." What do you think?

12

Natural Gas Production Should Be Increased

Peggy Williams

Peggy Williams is a certified petroleum geologist, an active member of the American Association of Petroleum Geologists, and the exploration editor for Oil and Gas Investor *magazine.*

The demand for natural gas in the United States is growing rapidly while production has remained stagnant. The nation needs gas for heating homes, generating electricity, and industrial purposes. Natural gas occurs in many wilderness regions in the mountains of the west. The gas industry, however, believes it can extract this fuel with minimal damage to the environment. While managing this wilderness for recreational value may be important, it is also imperative to the economy that natural gas production proceed in the Powder River Basin, Alaska, Nevada, Utah, and wildlands in other states.

From the great gas basins of the Rocky Mountains, to the seaboards of the Atlantic and Pacific coasts, to the northernmost reaches of arctic Alaska, battles are being fought between proponents of mineral extraction and advocates of nondevelopment. Debates rage over the amount of public land that should be available for energy production, and how that land should be protected.

The oil and gas industry points to its outstanding environmental record, and believes that it can help supply the nation's vital energy needs while carefully preserving the environment. Not surprisingly, another camp vehemently disputes this contention.

Underpinning the industry's urgency is the projected growth in energy demand. In its "Annual Energy Outlook 2002," the U.S. Energy Information Administration estimates the nation's total energy consumption will increase more rapidly than domestic energy production through 2020. Petroleum production is expected to decline 0.2% per year to some 5.6 million barrels per day in 2020. The swelling demand will push net oil imports from 53% of consumption in 2000 to 62% in 2020.

At the same time, U.S. gas production is expected to increase significantly, jumping from 52.3 billion cubic feet (Bcf) per day in 2000 to 78 Bcf per day in 2020, an average annual growth rate of 2%. That will not be enough to meet anticipated demand, however, and gas imports are forecast to rise from 9.6 Bcf per day in 2000 to 15 Bcf per day in 2020.

Whether the nation's drillers can actually supply this gas is an open question, however. Supply is almost wholly domestic, and a considerable resource base lies on lands controlled by the federal government.

"We are currently undergoing a transition in gas supply from domestic sources," says Mark Papa, chairman and chief executive officer of Houston-based EOG Resources. For the past 10 years, the U.S. supply has been remarkably stable, running around 52 Bcf per day, plus or minus 1 Bcf. But, U.S. gas production is declining at an ever-sharper rate, dropping steeply from a 16% annual decline in 1990 to an estimated 29% in 2002. ". . . An almost unprecedented decline in U.S. gas production is occurring."

"We see a severe constriction in the supply available to the U.S. gas market during the next several years."

Shutting off access to public lands

And, at the same time supply is significantly constricting, environmental groups are working intensively to shut off access to public lands. Indeed, in three offshore areas—the eastern Gulf of Mexico and the Atlantic and Pacific seaboards—new federal leasing of oil and gas rights is prohibited by moratoria. President George H.W. Bush signed an executive memorandum in 1990 placing a 10-year moratorium on new leasing off much of the nation's coast; President Clinton renewed and extended the moratorium to 2012.

An exception to the ban on new leases is one portion of the eastern Gulf south of Gulf Shores, Alabama, which had been part of a strategic plan for many years and already contained 23 blocks under lease. After a firestorm of protest from Florida, the [George W.] Bush administration sliced the size of the eastern Gulf sale, held in December 2001, by 75% to 1.5 million acres.

Another heated battle of late was the effort to open portions of the Arctic National Wildlife Refuge [ANWR], adjacent to Prudhoe Bay on Alaska's North Slope. In April 2002, the U.S. Senate defeated a plan to allow oil exploration in ANWR; the [George W.] Bush administration had strongly advocated that exploration as part of its national energy plan.

The Senate refusal to allow oil and gas leasing in ANWR and the withdrawal of 4.4 million acres from the eastern Gulf sale are both perceived by environmentalists as stunning successes, and those groups are now turning their attention to the next target—the Rocky Mountain region, says Marc Himmelstein, president of Washington-based lobbying firm Nation Environmental Strategies. The Beltway firm handles issues in the environmental and energy fields, working with such entities as the Departmental Protection Agency and Department of Energy.

The Bureau of Land Management [BLM] administers surface activities on some 262 million acres of federal land, and subsurface mineral estates on 700 million acres. Most of these lands are in the 12 Western states, including Alaska—some 84% of the subsurface minerals in Nevada are federally owned, as are 67% of Wyoming and Utah's mineral estates, 46% of New Mexico's and 44% of Colorado's.

A mosaic of regulations already governs oil and gas development in the federal onshore, with constraints ranging from no access at all, to seasonal restrictions on activity, to complex federal permitting requirements.

But, environmentalist are also throwing any obstacle they can in the way of oil and gas development on federal lands—challenging individual permits to drill, existing leases, future lease sales, environmental impact statements, environmental assessments, and resource-management plans, says Himmelstein. "We face lawsuits at every step of the way."

Broad-based attacks against energy development

The Rocky Mountain region is the new poster child for the environmental movement, agrees Jim Sims, executive director of Denver-based Western Business Roundtable. "Eastern-based environmental groups are preparing a broad-based attack against energy and resource development in the region."

Although the health and vitality of the West depend to a large degree on the health and vitality of its energy and resource-development industries, that linkage is not clear to many of today's Westerners. A heterogeneous mix of ranchers, developers, retirees, and vacation-home owners populates the rural areas; sometimes they own surface rights but not the underlying oil and gas estates. When an oil or gas well is proposed, they can be very alarmed.

Too, while environmental groups have strong grassroots organizations and effective public relations campaigns, like attempts by the industry have not been nearly as fruitful. Indeed, the industry's efforts to portray itself as a valuable contributor to local economies, as a responsible steward of the environment, and as a sector essential to national security have failed to engage the public.

"An almost unprecedented decline in U.S. gas production is occurring."

Moreover, some organizations are actively opposed to the energy industry's message. While many environmental groups are reasonable advocates of their positions, another set goes beyond advocacy to extremes. Members of the more extreme groups have a hard time seeing the West as an economic development region.

"Certain of these groups have not just an antidevelopment philosophy, but also a political strategy that is designed to force fundamental economic and lifestyle changes through dramatic increases in conventional energy prices," says Sims.

During the next several years, there will be many votes in Congress that are aimed at locking up sections of the West from development. Part of these will be through creation of national parks and monuments; others will be through riders and amendments to appropriation bills that will try to do a little here and a little there. "Politically, these kinds of votes are easy to force, and they are difficult to vote against."

Sims is organizing "Save the Rockies Coalition," a group that is reaching beyond the extractive industries to include many of the region's diverse constituencies. "We want to rally the West against what we see as direct attacks on our economy by groups that are largely based in the East. Public lands must be available for public use, and domestic energy development is good for both the region's economic health and for the nation's security."

Complicated federal requirements

The coalbed-methane [CBM] play [project] in the Powder River Basin is front and center in today's public lands controversy. Here, operators, local citizens, national and local environmental groups and various federal agencies are wrestling with how public lands should be used and protected.

Drilling operations are being delayed while the industry awaits final environmental impact statements [EIS] in both Wyoming and Montana. Draft statements, one for Wyoming and one for Montana, were issued May 15 [2002].

Presently, no federal permits are being issued in Wyoming's Powder River CBM play, with the exception of a few . . . locations. . . . Permits for conventional wells on federal lands are also affected, because they too have reached their threshold of activity. The impact is tremendous, as the BLM controls more than 60% of the oil and gas rights in the CBM play, although it handles just 10% of the surface.

"Eastern-based environmental groups are preparing a broad-based attack against energy and resource development in the region."

Wyoming's draft EIS, covering impacts for the potential development of as many as 51,000 wells by 2010, is being reworked at present. The regional office of the EPA came out against the BLM's preferred alternative, saying that choice would render the Tongue and Belle Fourche rivers unsuitable for irrigation. The agency was also concerned with air quality and the impacts of the development on fish and wildlife.

In Montana, no permits for CBM drilling—on federal, state or free lands—are being issued at all, outside of a restricted number allowed under a prior settlement agreement. Montana decided to pursue a statewide EIS for CBM development.

The EPA also found problems with Montana's Draft EIS. It believed the document did not clearly spell out how watersheds would be protected from degradation, and that it did not sufficiently analyze the impacts of development on air quality, tribal life, groundwater and wildlife.

"In the Powder River Basin, we are finding that a traditional EIS is no longer being used," says Himmelstein. Previously, the EIS was a broad-based document that looked at broad impacts over a large geographic area. "Some of the things EPA is proposing, and the environmentalists are pushing even further, are to consider the EIS a localized document for each and every individual lease and well. When you are dealing with the potential of 50,000-plus wells, it is impossible, impractical and not required by the law to be that precise."

> *"The nation clearly needs to reach a balance*
> *between meeting environmental goals and obtaining*
> *gas supply."*

Currently, the BLM is addressing comments from the federal agencies, state agencies and the public on the drafts for both states. Optimistically, the final EIS documents are expected prior to year-end. After each is issued, a 30-day public comment period will be held. Comments generated during those periods will subsequently be evaluated by the BLM. A "Record of Decision" [ROD] is the final step, and can be expected as quickly as a month after the close of the comment period or as long as a year later.

Still, these are regional EIS documents, and site-specific National Environmental Policy Act analyses will also be required for drilling permits, notes Joe Icenogle, government affairs specialist for Fidelity Exploration & Production Co., a subsidiary of MDU Resources Group. "Some people have the misconception that once the ROD is issued, we'll have a shotgun start to development. That is just not the situation."

A challenging bureaucracy

Even on public lands where oil and gas development is allowed, and the environmental assessments and impact statements have been approved and finalized, securing federal permits can take a great deal of time. Clearly, many in the industry are frustrated by the complexity and slow pace of the process.

"It's a challenge to be in the oil and gas business if your leases are on federal lands, due to a number of factors," says John Northington, vice president of Nation Environmental Strategies. "Part of it is just the bureaucracy."

At a . . . symposium sponsored by the Rocky Mountain Association of Geologists and Denver Geophysical Society in early 2002, Stuart Wright, a geophysical advisor with WesternGeco, noted that companies should optimistically plan on four to five months to obtain a federal permit for seismic [surveys] on lands administered by the BLM. The Federal process includes filing a notice of intent to obtain permission to survey the area, a biological survey, an archeological survey, and a review of the permit by the state's historic preservation office. Native American groups also may have to be notified, and a 30-day public comment period is required.

After the permit is secured, actual acquisition for a small survey might take another 15 to 40 days. But, restrictions for winter range activity, raptor nesting, sage grouse strutting, elk calving and hunting seasons can shrink the time available for that work to a period from August to mid-November.

Drilling permits can be equally as arduous to obtain. Bill White, vice president and chief financial officer for Midland-based Pure Resources Inc., says his firm has had problems obtaining federal permits. "We have federal leases in the San Juan Basin, and when we tried to get permits they would be turned down."

The company came up against interpretational differences between what it believed was stated by the regulations and how the local BLM offices interpreted those regulations. In one case, the field office of the BLM had a rule that a location had to be within 300 feet of a road. That particular guideline was not provided for in the regulations, and the company was eventually successful in having the guideline set aside.

Pure's approach is to foster relationships with the regulators that recognize both sides of the issues. "We have a very thorough understanding of the regulations, and we know the regulators very well and understand where they are coming from.

"Often, the lease stipulations are totally subject to the local BLM jurisdictions. A lot of the interpretations are a function of the political and environmental stances of the individuals involved in the process. Bureaucracies can certainly be arbitrary."

Nonetheless, there is some positive movement. "During the past two appropriation cycles—and if the Interior Department appropriations move forward, a third consecutive year—Congress has increased resources provided to process leases, to review the environmental impacts and to provide enforcement," says Himmelstein. Those actions will potentially speed up the industry's capability to access the nation's natural gas.

The issue remaining will be the perennial one of economics, and included in the economics will be an operator's estimation of what it will cost to continually fight the environmentalist. "They are not going to go away," he adds.

Still, significant volumes of untapped gas reserves reside in the Rocky Mountain area, and it is one of the only domestic areas that can grow its production. "The nation clearly needs to reach a balance between meeting environmental goals and obtaining gas supply, and we that that can be accomplished," says EOG's Papa.

13

Off-Road Vehicles Are Degrading the Wilderness

Keith Easthouse

Keith Easthouse is associate editor of Forest Magazine, *published by the Forest Service Employees for Environmental Ethics.*

Until 1988 motorized vehicles wider than forty inches were banned from National Forest trails. When this obscure "forty-inch rule" was lifted, it opened wilderness trails to snowmobiles, four-wheel all-terrain vehicles, and other off-road vehicles (ORVs). Since that time, many formerly peaceful and serene trails have become noisy, polluted highways. Motorized use has despoiled the wilderness character with the whine of loud engines, the stench of burning fuel, and the pollution of dripping gas, oil, and antifreeze. Powerful ORVs have not only degraded thousands of miles of trails but have allowed users to tear up hillsides, mountaintops, streams, and other fragile ecosystems. Study after study has shown that ORVs are harming plants and animals in a variety of ways and are even responsible for pushing endangered species toward extinction in some places. Despite this negative news, off-road groups, often with the backing of the ORV industry, continue to push the Forest Service to open new lands to motorized recreation. They have also fought nearly every attempt to limit ORVs in threatened areas. While the wilderness managers try to please as many visitors as possible, people riding ORVs are creating noise, air, and water pollution while driving hikers, horseback riders, hunters, and fishermen out of the wilderness.

In the September 14, 1988, issue of the *Federal Register*, a publication that records and communicates the rules and regulations of the executive branch of government, there appeared a notice from the U.S. Forest Service on page 35,526: the agency was proposing to lift its long standing rule prohibiting vehicles wider than forty inches from using national forest [trails]. The stated purpose of changing the rule, which had made it illegal to drive anything larger than a dirt bike on hiking and horse trails,

Keith Easthouse, "Out of Control," *Forest Magazine*, May/June 2000. Copyright © 2000 by *Forest Magazine*. Reproduced by permission.

was to "eliminate confusion and law enforcement difficulties."

The plan to abolish "the forty inch rule," as the regulation is known, was remarkable in how little public controversy it generated. The Forest Service received a total of five public comments and prepared a cursory, two-and-a-half page environmental analysis that concluded that revoking the rule "will not have a significant effect on the human environment." On November 11, 1989, then Forest Service Chief F. Dale Robertson signed the decision notice approving the rule change, and on June 25 of the following year, the final rule went into effect.

The lack of public controversy over the rule change stood in sharp contrast to reactions within the agency. Internal documents obtained in 1998 by the Montana Wilderness Association, an environmental group, show that many land managers were alarmed. "Allowing wider vehicles to use trails may cause trails to become roads," asserted an employee from Region 9, which encompasses the upper Midwest and the New England states. Another Forest Service worker, this one from Indiana's Hoosier National Forest, warned that removing the rule "would generate strong negative reaction from the public. It would be viewed as another step in opening up the forest to unrestricted ORV [off-road vehicle] use."

Some in the agency apparently saw the hand of the ORV industry behind the proposal. William L. Nickbush, recreation officer on the Mark Twain National Forest in Missouri, wrote in a February 6, 1986, memo that "our responsibility is to the land and its protection. We don't believe we need to accommodate every type vehicle just because someone manufactures it and someone else bought it and wants to use it." Bruce Hronek, director of Recreation, Range, Wildlife and Landscape Management on the Chequamegon National Forest in Wisconsin, agreed: "We see no justification for continually altering our definition of a trail to suit corporate decisions to manufacture larger and larger snowmobiles, ATVs [all-terrain vehicles], or other motorized vehicles."

Trails opened to off-road vehicles

Top Forest Service officials to this day deny that ORV groups improperly influenced the agency's decision to rescind the forty-inch rule. They also insist that the plan was widely publicized—a claim environmentalists refute. Whatever the case, one thing is clear: the ORV community knew the Forest Service was considering doing away with the rule at least two years before the initial Federal Register notice. In the pile of documents obtained by Montana environmentalists was a September 30, 1986, letter written by Bob Garner of the Montana Trail Bike Riders Association to then–Forest Service Chief R. Max Peterson. The letter begins: "It has come to our association's attention through discussions with the Forest Service Regional Office in Missoula, Montana, that a review of [the forty-inch] regulation is taking place." Later in the letter, Garner baldly asserted that "redefining a trail and correcting the inadvertent exclusion of ATV riders clearly is necessary at this time. Arbitrary limitations such as the forty-inch-width regulations have a serious negative impact on motorcycle and ATV dealers selling these vehicles."

The forty-inch rule was far from arbitrary—it was based on the width of a motorcycle's handlebar—and as the alarmed Forest Service land managers warned, rescinding it did indeed open up trails to four-wheel-drive ATVs and snowmobiles.

More than a decade later, such vehicles—made more powerful by recent technological advancements—are pushing deeper into the backcountry than ever before, not only in national forests but also in national parks and in lands administered by the Bureau of Land Management.

Outraged environmental groups, claiming that the machines are harassing wildlife and tearing up the land, are filing lawsuits—and seeking political support from the Clinton administration. ORV enthusiasts, claiming they are being discriminated against, are fighting every attempt to ban their machines from pristine areas—and looking to the Republican-controlled Congress to advance their cause. Meanwhile, the Forest Service, which opened the floodgates to ORVs on its own lands by nixing the forty-inch rule, finds itself in the middle of yet another environmental battle, one that could potentially be as bitter and protracted as the timber wars.

Perhaps more bitter and protracted: this conflict doesn't pit the public against the resource extraction industry but recreation users against each other. As Forest Service Chief Mike Dombeck, a man not given to overstatement, put it recently, "This will be the issue of the next decade."

Motorized recreation is growing rapidly

There's no question the chances are growing greater that your next outdoor experience may be shattered by the deep roar of a four-wheeler or the angry-hornet whine of a Jet Ski.

Motorized recreation on public lands seems to be growing rapidly, but it's not clear by how much. Although individual national forests may track ORV use, the Forest Service keeps no comprehensive figures. The agency has estimated that ORV visitor days will reach 118 million by 2020, although some within the Forest Service believe that figure has already been reached.

There are several factors driving the increase: the growing tendency of Americans to turn to nature when they want to have fun; an increasing number of Americans with money to burn, thanks to the unprecedented economic boom [of the late 1990s]; and a growing number of Americans who have hit middle age and are less inclined to strap on their hiking boots and break a sweat. Add to these demographic trends the fact that the motorized recreation industry is churning out bigger and more powerful machines than ever before and you have a peculiarly American phenomenon: wilderness traffic jams.

"It used to be that if you had a snowmachine and you really wanted to get out there, you took your shovel and snowshoes with you because you knew you were going to get stuck," said Robert Ekey, who works in the Wilderness Society's Bozeman, Montana, office. "But now these machines have a broader track and a platform so they don't sink in the snow anymore. Places that only skiers used to be able to reach are now all tracked up by snowmachines."

Harried hikers and skiers aren't the only outcome of the ORV boom. The abundance of machines roaring through the backcountry has taken a tangible toll on wildlife and the environment in general. Solid information on ORV impacts on national forests is difficult to come by, largely because the Forest Service—contrary to its own regulations—does very little monitoring. But there is scientifically documented evidence of negative impacts outside national forests. Here are a few examples:

In the Mojave National Preserve in Southern California, a number of species, including the endangered desert tortoise and the desert kangaroo rat, have suffered hearing loss from the roar of dune buggies. Some of the rats were found to have bloody ears and to have been deafened for as long as three weeks—a period during which they were extremely vulnerable to predation by their main enemy, snakes.

> *"We don't believe we need to accommodate every type vehicle just because someone manufactures it and someone else bought it and wants to use it."*

In the Back Bay National Wildlife Refuge in Virginia, ORV use in the 1970s decimated the ghost crab population, reduced the number of sanderlings—a shore bird—from 30,000 to 5,000 and compacted the sand so densely that sea turtles could not establish nesting sites.

In Canyonlands National Park, ORV users tore up an eleven-mile stretch of Salt Creek, the only clear perennial stream in the park. The machines left fuel, oil and antifreeze in the canyon bottom and damaged habitat for the Southwestern willow flycatcher, an endangered songbird.

A nonnative root fungus that is fatal to a rare conifer called the Port Orford cedar, found mostly in southern Oregon, is spread readily by motorized vehicles, which transport spores on their tires. An environmental group called Friends of the Kalmiopsis claims that ORVs regularly trespass into the wilderness, where the fungus has killed hundreds of the cedars in recent years.

A study in Montana found that a single ATV can disperse more than 2,000 knapweed seeds over a ten-mile radius. Knapweed, in contrast to most native vegetation in Montana, thrives in soils compressed by the weight of ATVs.

A study in the early 1980s found that runoff in the Southern California desert was as much as twenty times greater in areas where soil was compacted by ATVs.

Damage from snowmobiles

Some of the dirtiest air in the country hangs at the western entrance to Yellowstone National Park, where snowmobiles congregate. The highest carbon monoxide level recorded anywhere in the United States in 1996 was recorded at West Yellowstone.

Several studies have found that even though snowmobiles do not directly impact soil, they still damage vegetation. Compressed snow caused by the machines' weight produces colder subsurface temperatures that reduce plant vigor come springtime. The compressed snow also harms and even kills small rodents that spend the winter in burrows.

Fuel and motor oil leaked by snowmobiles during the winter in alpine regions of the northern Rockies has been found to produce a poisonous pulse of snowmelt in the springtime, resulting in the deaths of aquatic species.

A study of white-tailed deer in the Rockies in the mid-1980s found that the animals used up vital energy reserves trying to escape snowmobiles. Another study later that decade found that harassment of mule deer by ATVs resulted in reduced reproduction rates.

According to the U.S. Fish and Wildlife Service, the hardening of snow produced by snowmobiles decreases the competitive advantage of the Canada lynx, a protected species that is adapted to deep snow.

Wolverines, an imperiled species found only in remote areas, have abandoned their dens when faced with minor human disturbances, according to a study done in the 1960s. Conservationists speculate that wolverines, not to mention grizzly bears and wolves, are severely taxed by ORVs—not only in winter but at all times of year.

Evidence such as this helps explain why environmentalists get a tad emotional about ORV use on public lands—and more than a little angry when it comes to what they perceive to be weak or nonexistent regulation of ORV use by land management agencies.

"If your idea of Forest Service management is a bad scene from [the film] *Road Warrior*, then that's what we've got out there. Chaos. Entire trail systems are being destroyed."

ORV enthusiasts, claiming they are being discriminated against, are fighting every attempt to ban their machines from pristine areas.

So says John Gatchell of the Montana Wilderness Association, the group that brought the agency's internal deliberations on the cancellation of the forty-inch rule to light. The association, established in 1958, is Montana's oldest conservation group. It was also one of the first to recognize the danger posed to public lands by escalating ORV use.

In 1996, at a time when most environmental organizations were still focused on logging, mining and grazing, the association filed a lawsuit alleging Forest Service mismanagement of seven wilderness study areas totaling some 700,000 acres, all in the Big Sky State. The suit charged the agency with violating the Montana Wilderness Study Act of 1977, a federal law meant to ensure that areas pristine enough to eventually gain formal wilderness designation remain protected. The Forest Service was degrading the wild character of these areas, according to the suit, primarily by creating and expanding trails for ATVs and grooming trails for snowmobiles.

In a federal district court hearing last spring, Assistant U.S. Attorney Deanne Sandholm, representing the Forest Service, did not deny that the agency was accommodating motorized recreation in potential wilderness areas. Nor did she deny that such use carries a high risk of degrading the environment. But she argued that such use does not necessarily preclude wilderness designation. The agency is handling the issue of ORV activity in wilderness study areas—which exist on national forests across the country—on a case-by-case basis, she said. In some wilderness study areas in Montana, she said, motorized use is off-limits.

The lawsuit, which is still pending, is significant in many ways aside from being one of the first major challenges of Forest Service management of ORVs. It reveals that the agency was aiding and abetting an intensive—Gatchell would say destructive—form of recreation on lands that are among the most pristine under its jurisdiction. It shows that Forest Service engineers who formerly built logging roads are now building ORV routes ("miniroads," Gatchell calls them), without any public review or detailed study of potential impacts to the environment or wildlife. Finally, the lawsuit makes clear that when it comes to ORV use, the Forest Service has no uniform policy that applies to all of its wilderness study areas, let alone to all of its national forests.

Bid to manage ORVs

A lack of consistency lies at the heart of another, more recent challenge to the Forest Service's handling of ORVs: a bid by environmentalists to persuade the agency to fundamentally change the way it manages the machines. The challenge, mounted by the Wilderness Society; the Wildlands Center for Preventing Roads, a Montana group; and 100 other environmental groups, takes the form of a 180-page "rule-making petition" that was submitted to the agency last December. The petition asks the agency to ban ORVs from the roughly 54 million acres of unprotected roadless areas in the 192-million-acre national forest system. It also asks the agency to allow the vehicles only on designated and signed routes and only where the agency can show that the vehicles will not cause undue environmental harm.

Currently, the Forest Service has no uniform policy addressing ORV use. Some forests restrict ORVs to designated routes; others do just the opposite, allowing ORVs to travel everywhere except in areas that have been closed off.

Mike Anderson, a Wilderness Society lawyer based in Seattle, said in March that Forest Service officials have indicated they are not likely to respond to the petition anytime soon (a response is required by law, but there is no deadline by which a response must be made). "They've told us there's too much on their plate," Anderson said.

> *"If your idea of Forest Service management is a bad scene from* Road Warrior, *then that's what we've got out there. Chaos. Entire trail systems are being destroyed."*

That's understandable, considering the agency is in the midst of preparing a controversial proposal to protect its roadless areas, as directed by President Clinton [in 1999] in a much ballyhooed announcement. But even in the absence of other priorities, it seems unlikely that the agency will meet the environmentalists' demands.

Chris Wood, an aide to Dombeck, said the question of where off-road vehicles should be allowed is best left to local forest supervisors. But in those places where ORV users have created unauthorized trails—a rampant problem, environmentalists say—Dombeck wants forest supervisors to limit vehicle use to designated areas, Wood said.

Dombeck, in a speech last October, stressed the need for public review of plans regarding ORVs, something called for in the petition: "Off-road vehicle use decisions will be made through an open and public process unless there is justifiable need for immediate action to protect forest resources or public safety," Dombeck said.

He also sided with environmentalists on another issue—that the Forest Service must stop sanctioning, with no public review, illegally created routes. "Any decision to make currently unauthorized roads and trails a part of the authorized forest road and transportation system will be made through open and public processes," Dombeck said.

Although environmentalists praised the speech, they have been disappointed by the lack of response to the petition. And while no one from the environmental community will say so at this point, it seems likely that they will eventually go to court to try to force the agency to adopt more severe restrictions on ORV use.

Anderson said a lawsuit might charge the agency with violating its own regulations, which include restrictions that grew out of a pair of executive orders issued in the 1970s by presidents Nixon and Carter. The orders direct all land management agencies to "protect the resources of those lands, to promote the safety of all users, and to minimize conflicts among the various users of those lands."

Opposition from pro-ORV groups

Clark Collins, executive director of the Blue Ribbon Coalition, the largest pro-ORV group, has no doubt that the Wilderness Society and the other petitioners will go to court. He also is certain of something else: what environmentalists—he calls them "wilderness advocates"—really want to convert as much backcountry as possible to protected wilderness.

Some might see that as a laudable goal. But Collins says it smacks of "selfishness" and "elitism." "It's been their position all along that any area of scenic or recreational value should be closed to motorized recreation. They want to lock us out."

When asked if ORVs damage the backcountry, Collins suggested that horses are more destructive. (The leader of a Montana ORV club made a similar remark recently, claiming that hiking was more disruptive to grizzlies than motorized recreation. The proof? More hiker's are mauled than ORV riders. An environmentalist retorted, "It's hard to surprise a grizzly on an ATV.")

Even if ORVs do harm the land, Collins said, local ORV clubs are quite active in their efforts to repair the damage by maintaining trails and roads that the Forest Service and the Bureau of Land Management cannot afford to maintain themselves.

Wood, Dombeck's aide, agreed. "The environmental community hates to hear this, but some of our best partners, some of the people that show up most often to do volunteer work on weekends, who leverage more money for us for maintenance work, are the OHV [off-highway vehicle] clubs. We don't turn up our nose at that. They're organized, they turn out people, they help cash-strapped forests. The work they do helps stop erosion."

Money for such maintenance work, however, doesn't come out of the pockets of ORV clubs; it comes from American taxpayers through a 1991 law known as the Symms Act, named for its main sponsor, former Senator Steve Symms, an Idaho Republican and ally of the Blue Ribbon Coalition, based in Pocatello, Idaho.

The act funds trail construction and maintenance through a gasoline tax distributed by the states. In theory, 30 percent of the money is reserved for building and maintaining motorized roads, 30 percent is to be spent on hiking and horse trails, and the remainder—40 percent—is supposed to go toward "multiple use." In practice, the bulk of the multiple-use portion of the fund has been spent on projects benefiting ORV groups.

Environmentalists say the fund gives the Forest Service an incentive to do the bidding of the ORV community. They also complain about a provision in the act that allows Forest Service land managers to widen trails without public review. (Perhaps the most extreme incident occurred last year on the Dixie National Forest in Utah, when a district ranger—at the behest of local ATV users—widened a horse and hiking trail with a small bulldozer. After environmentalists complained, he was ordered to restore the trail to its original condition.) And conservationists were aghast, though not surprised, when congressional Republicans not only resurrected the bill [in the summer of 1999]—it lapsed in 1997—but pushed through legislation that will provide $270 million over the next five years to build new ORV routes and shore up old ones on national forests and BLM lands.

Victories for environmentalists

Not all the news is bad for those seeking more restrictions on ORV use on public lands.

Yellowstone National Park, perhaps the Mecca for snowmobile enthusiasts, is leaning toward banning the machines altogether. The BLM, long criticized for doing even less than the Forest Service to control ORV use, in January unveiled an initiative to develop a "national strategy for ensuring environmentally responsible [ORV] use." (Perhaps not coincidentally, the announcement came a few months after a coalition of environmental groups sued the agency for failing to control ORVs in the spectacular canyon country of southern Utah.) And the Fish and Wildlife Service's decision in March to list the Canada lynx as threatened could conceivably lead to a moratorium on new groomed snowmobile routes in lynx habitat. At the very least, the listing gives environmentalists an important legal weapon to wield.

A clear cut victory was achieved in February when a federal judge rejected a bid by a Montana snowmobile organization to reopen fourteen western Montana roadless areas on the Lolo National Forest.

The Montana Snowmobile Association claimed the forest should have held public hearings before closing about 400,000 acres to motorized uses last year. However Judge Donald Molloy ruled that the Forest Service had already held public hearings back in 1986, when the ban was incorporated into the Lolo's management plan.

Gatchell of the Montana Wilderness Association said that while the ruling was welcome, the snowmobile group initiated the lawsuit only because Lolo officials largely ignored their forest plan for thirteen years and then belatedly enforced the ban after Gatchell's group threatened to sue them if they didn't.

"If they'd only implemented the ban from the beginning, none of this would have happened," Gatchell said.

"On every visit to the trail system, I find new trespass and resource damage. We cannot meet our mission to protect watersheds and allow this type of use to continue."

Last December, environmentalists added another win to their tally when the Wenatchee National Forest in Washington backed away from a plan to build a six-mile-long dirt bike trail from a campground to a road-less area. The cancellation followed a court ruling ordering the forest to look at the cumulative impact on the environment of its entire trail system before proceeding.

Although there is plenty of evidence of pro-ORV bias within the Forest Service, the agency has taken some steps to curb ORV use: In 1994, the Idaho Panhandle National Forests closed fourteen square miles of the Selkirk Mountains to protect endangered woodland caribou.

Colorado's Routt National Forest has closed 250,000 acres to motorized recreation an action that is being challenged in court by the Colorado OHV Coalition.

The Dixie National Forest in Utah has closed ninety miles of trails and roads in a scenic but badly degraded alpine area known as Boulder Top. For that step they have also been sued by ORV groups claiming that the Forest Service is discriminating against people with disabilities who can reach the area only on motorized vehicles.

The Grand Mesa, Uncompahgre and Gunnison National Forests, which cover 1.7 million acres in western Colorado, along with the Gunnison District of the BLM, which manages 600,000 acres, are proposing to restrict motorized vehicles and mountain bikes—both of which have heavily impacted the mountainous region.

Managers with the Hoosier National Forest in Indiana and the Monongahela National Forest in West Virginia have banned ORVs entirely.

On other fronts, environmental groups recently sued Montana's Gallatin National Forest for failing to halt ORV caused destruction of grizzly hear habitat (grizzlies are a threatened species). And in February, a Missouri-based group called Heartwood turned to the courts in a bid to halt the opening of thirty-four miles of ORV trails in Kentucky's Daniel Boone National Forest. (In 1998, that national forest confined ORVs to 117 of the forest's 500 miles of trails. Prior to that, ORVs were permitted to travel cross-country.)

Conflicts will escalate

Dombeck is on record saying that in this day and age, the Forest Service's top priority should be protecting the integrity of watersheds. That means, as he has repeatedly explained, keeping the air and water clean, maintaining good wildlife habitat and ensuring that significant portions of the national forest system remain places of serenity.

But he is also bound by law to manage national forests to satisfy multiple uses. Like it or not, for a growing number of Americans, one of those multiple uses is driving through the woods on a four-wheeler or zipping through a winter meadow on a powerful snowmobile.

Therein lies Dombec's dilemma. . . . But it seems safe to say that court battles will escalate, as will conflicts between hikers, hunters amid anglers on the one hand and ORV riders on the other. In the meantime, the predictions of trouble that some Forest Service land managers gave voice to when the agency was mulling whether to do away with the forty inch rule fourteen years ago have largely come true.

Perhaps it is fitting, then, to let a Forest Service employee, one Marsha Lee Winkle of the Wayne National Forest in Ohio, have the last word. A letter she wrote to her superiors on October 29, 1998, is often cited by environmentalists. It reads, in part: "I am disheartened by our inability to control ORV users. On every visit to the trail system, I find new trespass and resource damage. We cannot meet our mission to protect watersheds and allow this type of use to continue."

14

Off-Road Vehicles Should Be Allowed to Use Wilderness Areas

Jeff Henson

Jeff Henson is an off-road enthusiast and the desert editor for ATV Illustrated *magazine.*

The Endangered Species Act (ESA) is a loosely written law that sometimes uses inexact science to list a species as threatened. Environmentalists have wrongly used the ESA to close off huge tracts of land to logging, mining, and off-road vehicle (ORV) use. In the Imperial Sand Dunes in southeastern California, the Bureau of Land Management has locked ORVs out of thousands of acres by claiming that a plant called Pierson's milkvetch is threatened. An independent scientific review has disputed these findings, but this report has not stopped the environmental lobby. In an attempt to turn public opinion against motorized recreation, environmentalists have used a few cases of illegal behavior at the dunes to demonize law-abiding ORV users in the press. While the controversy rages over the ecological health of the milkvetch, responsible off-road riders should not be banned from public lands that are supposed to be managed for multiple use by the public.

Are you one of the hundreds of thousands of off-road vehicle users who consider sand dune recreational areas your home away from home? Do you spend the majority of your holiday weekends cresting dune after dune, racing up the tallest hills, then sharing your adventures with your family and friends around the campfire at night? Do you feel this experience strengthens the bonds between you and your loved ones? Well then, you might like to know a little about the so-called environmental groups that plan to yank this experience away from you—and the negative picture they are painting of you in the process. . . .

In March 2000, the Tucson-based Center for Biological Diversity (CBD), Sierra Club and Public Employees for Environmental Responsibility (PEER) joined forces and sued the California Bureau of Land Management (BLM), claiming that the BLM failed to consult with the U.S. Fish and Wildlife Service (FWS) as required by Section 7 of the Endangered Species Act. Written in 1973, the ESA was established to protect animal and plant species when their numbers render them prone to possible extinction. With all of its good intentions, the ESA is a very broadly written federal law, with many gray areas. It allows anyone to petition the FWS to have a species listed or reclassified as threatened or endangered based on "the best available science" rather than requiring science that stands up to critical peer review. This leaves the ESA wide open to abuse from special interest groups such as the CBD, Sierra Club and PEER. These groups are jointly attempting to use this loosely written law in an effort to completely ban off-road vehicle use (even, in many areas, mountain bikes!) within the nine-million-acre California Desert Conservation Area. Surprisingly, the BLM opted to avoid going to trial and agreed to settle out of court—with no public input.

Sand sport recreationalists avoid vegetation because their paddle tires are extremely prone to puncture.

The settlement listed several locations to be temporarily closed to off-road vehicle use until the consultation was complete. Included was 49,310 acres of the Imperial Sand Dunes Recreation Area in Southern California, more popularly known as Glamis. This closure is an addition to the 32,000 acres of dunes that make up the North Algodones Dunes Wilderness, located north of Highway 78. A plant known as Pierson's milkvetch is the reason for this closure. The environmentalists claim that this plant's numbers are declining due to constant trampling from off-road vehicles. They make this assertion in spite of the fact that Pierson's milkvetch also grows in the 32,000-acre wilderness area and is heavily dependent on rainfall to sustain its numbers.

Plant not threatened

In the few short years since its birth, the American Sand Association [ASA] has made tremendous progress toward reversing the closures in the Imperial Sand Dunes area. One of the ASA's biggest accomplishments was the hiring of an independent biological consulting firm to complete a thorough analysis of the Pierson's milkvetch, as well as other species that environmental groups could attempt to use to further their agenda. In the spring of 2001, several ASA members volunteered their time and sand vehicles to transport the biologist across the entire open dune system. The biological team was able to determine that at least 71,926 individual plants exist in the areas currently open to ORV use (this figure does not include the plants in the closed areas or the wilderness area, because the team was not allowed to enter these locations with motorized vehicles; however, an aerial survey was taken of the closed area in which a large number of plants were observed). It is estimated that approximately 140,000 plants exist in the open and recently closed dunes (these figures don't include the number of plants in the wilderness area or the section of dunes that spill across the border into Mexico). This study also reconfirmed that the Pierson's milkvetch numbers fluctuate according to the amount of rainfall each year. It was determined that the plant's biggest foe is lack of water—not the paddle tires [with large flippers for traction in sand] of dune buggies, motorcycles and ATV's. Sand sport recreationalists avoid vegetation because their paddle tires are extremely prone to puncture. Of all the individual plants counted in the open riding areas, less than 1% were determined to have been damaged by off-road vehicles. This study is one that most definitely will stand up to critical peer review. The ASA feels that it clearly shows the Pierson's milkvetch is not endangered. Armed with this info the ASA, along with the San Diego Off-Road Coalition and the Off-Road Business Association, filed a petition with the United States Department of the Interior to have the Pierson's milkvetch removed from the list of endangered species.

The ASA also filed a lawsuit against the BLM to reopen the closed dunes after it was discovered that the BLM failed to follow federal guidelines and produce a required Environmental Assessment in order for it to move forward with the dune closure. . . . While the off-road groups were successful in getting the BLM to rescind the original closure, the agency scrambled to reclose the areas and follow the proper procedures, effectively bringing the off-road groups' lawsuit to a halt. The good news is the BLM completed the Environmental Assessment and the Pierson's milkvetch study that was paid for by the ASA has been made part of that record.

Name-calling, half-truths and outright lies

It's painfully obvious that the environmental groups involved in the Glamis closure have rarely, if ever, encountered the amount of resistance placed on them by the ASA in any of their many lawsuits. Realizing that it will take more than an obscure plant to rid the dunes of off-road vehicles, they have turned to name-calling, half-truths and outright lies to further their agenda.

Right out of the gate, the narrator calls off-road recreationalists "a dangerous breed of wildlife."

PEER, in cooperation with the Center for Biological Diversity, produced a video intended for public viewing entitled "Bottles, Throttles and Preservation—BLM's Desert Quagmire". Right out of the gate, the narrator calls off-road recreationalists "a dangerous breed of wildlife." The narrator also claims that vegetation and wildlife are being trampled in the recently closed areas due to illegal off-road trespassing. Even on the Thanksgiving Day weekend, traditionally the dunes' busiest time in that well over 100,000 people use them, there were fewer than 100 instances where vehicle tracks were spotted in the closed areas—and most of them reversed direction shortly after they entered the closed area, as if the operators realized their mistake. The viewer is shown a picture of a crushed desert tortoise, which was later proved not to have been killed by an off-road vehicle (sand dunes are not desert tortoise habitat in the first place).

We are then introduced to PEER spokesman Eric Wingerter, who claims, "The large part of them (off-roaders) have some anti-government hostilities, so it's a dangerous situation for the rangers." This statement might be true if the United States was the socialist country that most environmental extremists dream of it becoming. The video narrator proceeds to add to Eric's statement: "They (the Rangers) have been threatened at Algodones and attacked. A recent Department of Interior investigation concludes drug- and alcohol-related crimes make the Algodones unsafe for families. The report also recommends BLM Rangers be issued riot helmets, batons and gas masks for their own safety. ATVs run their headlights and ride the dunes all night, and the need for law enforcement goes on 24 hours." What she doesn't tell you is that the report goes on to say that it isn't the typical off-roader who is causing the problem. The majority of these acts occur only on the busiest holiday weekends and usually are isolated to nighttime activities at Competition Hill, located adjacent to Interstate 78. The highway provides easy access to that area for people whose vehicles cannot travel through the dunes. It's no secret that gang activity has become a growing problem at Competition Hill over the last five years, with very little intervention by law-enforcement officers. Legitimate off-roaders, more than anyone else, would like to see this problem eliminated. This is evident in the checkered flag program promoted by the ASA. Checkered flags are flown as a symbol of support for law enforcement in the dunes. The checkered flag pledge reads, "WE FLY IT AND LIVE BY IT! TRASH: WE pack it in and WE pack it out. ENFORCEMENT: WE live by the rules. WE support all law enforcement at the dunes. WE report major infractions. RESPECT FOR OTHER PEOPLE, SAFETY AND THE ENVIRONMENT: WE act in a responsible manner."

As usual, environmental extremists have raised hypocrisy to an art form.

The PEER video also introduces us to CBD desert ecologists and Earth First leader Daniel Patterson. Patterson goes on to say, "I see them hauling off people in handcuffs all day for things like drunk driving and drug offenses. . . ." Once again we're led to believe that the majority of ORV users at the dunes are criminals. This is an interesting statement for Patterson, who ran for the Arizona State Senate in the fall of 2000. Topping his list of core issues we find decriminalization of marijuana "for medical and responsible personal use and cultivation." It's hard to believe that someone who has run for political office on a platform of legalizing marijuana has never possessed it or consumed it. Besides, possession of marijuana is considered a "drug offense"—exactly the kind of "activity" Patterson says is so prevalent among off-roaders! As usual, environmental extremists have raised hypocrisy to an art form.

Asking for fairness

In response to the PEER video, the American Sand Association produced its own video. Rather than descend to the level of its opposition with name-calling and half-truths, the ASA introduces us to the real people who frequent the Imperial Sand Dunes: parents, grandparents, children, firefighters, business owners, the handicapped . . . Americans who have a right to responsibly use lands their tax dollars and recreational fees pay for!

We are also introduced to ASA president Jerry Seaver. "We need help with the politicians to take the time to look at the facts and make sure this is all being done in a fair way," says Seaver. "That's all we're asking for—fairness. We are voters. All we leave in the sand is tracks—and the first time the wind blows, those are gone."

15

Economic Sabotage Is the Only Way to Stop Destruction of the Wilderness

Earth Liberation Front

The Earth Liberation Front is an international underground movement consisting of autonomous groups of people who carry out direct actions against projects that harm the environment. Since 1997 ELF cells have carried out dozens of actions resulting in more than $150 million in damages.

The Earth Liberation Front (ELF) believes that the best way to stop wilderness destruction is through acts of carefully planned sabotage. While taking pains to ensure that no one is killed or injured, ELF uses arson in order to destroy houses, apartments, offices, and other building projects under construction in environmentally sensitive areas. When ELF activists torch construction sites, logging companies, and government buildings, it brings national press attention to the cause of saving the environment. ELF members believe that when a person or company will harm or obliterate a wilderness area, they have a duty to stop it using whatever means necessary as long as no human life is threatened.

The Earth Liberation Front (ELF) is an international underground organization that uses direct action in the form of economic sabotage to stop the exploitation and destruction of the natural environment.

It has been speculated that the group was founded in the early 1990s as an offshoot of Earth First in England. The ideology of the ELF spread to North America in the mid 1990s. In November 1997, the ELF officially claimed responsibility for the group's first action in North America. The claim of responsibility was sent to above ground supporters who released the information to the media. In the communiqué the ELF claimed credit for releasing wild horses and burning down a Bureau of Land Management Horse Corral near Burns, Oregon, on November 29, 1997. The communiqué appeared as follows,

Earth Liberation Front, *Frequently Asked Questions About the Earth Liberation Front*, 2001.

"The Bureau of Land Management (BLM) claims they are removing non-native species from public lands (aren't white Europeans also non-native?) but then they turn around and subsidize the cattle industry and place thousands of non-native domestic cattle on these same lands . . . to help halt the BLM's illegal and immoral business of rounding up wild horses from public lands and funneling them to slaughter. . . .

This hypocrisy and genocide against the horse nation will not go unchallenged! The practice of rounding up and auctioning wild horses must be stopped. The practice of grazing cattle on public lands must be stopped. The time to take action is now. From an investigation like the Associated Press' to writing the BLM to an action like ours, you can help stop the slaughter and save our Mother Earth. . . . "

If one individual or even one entire cell is captured by authorities, other individuals and cells will be free to continue their work as they operate independently and anonymously.

This action caused an estimated $450,000 in damages to the facility and 448 wild horses and 51 burros were set free.

Since November of 1997, there have been over two dozen major actions performed by the ELF in North America alone resulting in nearly $40 million in damages. . . .

[Since that time] actions have been taken by the ELF all across the United States, in Canada, throughout Europe, and in South America. The number of locations targeted by the ELF continues to increase.

How the organization is structured

The ELF is organized into autonomous cells which operate independently and anonymously from one another and the general public. The group does not contain a hierarchy or any sort of leadership. Instead the group operates under an ideology. If an individual believes in the ideology and follows a certain set of guidelines she or he can perform actions and become a part of the ELF.

This cell structure has been extremely effective in ensuring the continuation of the organization with minimal arrests. Law enforcement, particularly in North America are trained to recognize and deal with organizations that have a leader, a hierarchy and a central headquarters. The ELF does not contain any of these. Due to the autonomous and underground aspects of the ELF cells, an infiltration into a cell by no way means the entire movement will be stopped. If one individual or even one entire cell is captured by authorities, other individuals and cells will be free to continue their work as they operate independently and anonymously from one another.

The cell structure is a type of guerilla tactic which has been successfully employed by various movements around the world for ages. It can be a successful tactic when used properly against a greater military power.

It is next to impossible to estimate the number of ELF members internationally or even country by country. Since 1997, in the United States, the ELF actions have steadily increased and have appeared in a growing number of differing geographical areas. Therefore it is safe to assume the group continues to grow in size.

More and more people around the world are realizing the horrifying state of the environment and the extreme, continuous exploitation of people and life in general caused by the greedy individual wanting more numbers to appear in the bank account. Simultaneously people are becoming increasingly frustrated with the exhausted state sanctioned, legal means of social change because on their own they do not work.

If people are serious about stopping the destruction and exploitation of all life on the planet then they must also be serious about recognizing the need for a real direct action campaign and their own personal involvement.

One cell in the ELF can consist of just a few people who have the ability to cause extreme amounts of economic damage with just one action. It doesn't take a trained expert to become involved in the ELF, just individuals who really care about life on the planet to the degree that they want to take actions to protect it. Environmental protection is a matter of self defense and the ELF actions are a natural response to the very real threats to life on earth. . . .

What is the ideology of the ELF?

The ELF realizes that the destruction of life is not a mere random occurrence but a deliberate act of violence performed by those entities concerned with nothing more than pursuing extreme economic gain at any cost. With this realization in mind, the ELF maintains that it is only logical to work to remove the profit motive from killing the earth and all life on it.

Anyone seeking to create actual positive social and political change must reflect on past attempts throughout history to learn what worked, what didn't, and what can be taken to aid in the current pursuit. A refusal to make this reflection is also a refusal to make an honest life commitment to the cause of justice and protection of life on this planet.

The ELF recognizes that the popular environmental movement has failed miserably in its attempts to bring about the protection needed to stop the killing of life on this planet.

The ELF recognizes that the popular environmental movement has failed miserably in its attempts to bring about the protection needed to stop the killing of life on this planet. State sanctioned means of social change rarely on their own have and will have any real effect in obtaining the desired results. This is due to the obvious fact that the legal means of protest in solving grievances do little more than reinforce the same system which is a root of the problem. The state system is not going to allow any real change within it unless the state structure (government), big business, and finally the mainstream consumer society feels that change is really necessary. Yet it is this same state structure, big business, and consumer society that is directly responsible for the destruction of life on the planet for the sake of profit. When these entities have repeatedly demonstrated their prioritizing of monetary gain ahead of life, it is absolute foolishness to continue to ask them nicely for reform or revolution. Matters must be taken into the hands of the people who need to more and more step outside of this societal law to enforce natural law.

One definition of natural law refers to our dependence on the substances in the natural environment which enable all life to exist, primarily clean air, clean water, and clean soil. Clean air is needed for life to breathe, clean water is needed for life to drink, and clean soil is needed to grow food for life to eat. . . .

The ELF ideology maintains that it is the very social and political ideology in operation throughout the westernized countries that is creating the various injustices on this planet and ultimately the destruction of life. That ideology is capitalism and the mindset that allows it to exist. Capitalism and . . . the American Dream have long symbolized a form of economic opportunity and freedom. The idea that no matter who you were, if you worked hard all your life, you too could have the perfect husband or wife, the 2.3 kids, new BMW, the beach house on Maui and penthouse in New York City and loads of cash to play with.

What wasn't and still isn't told to the millions seeking the American Dream is that dream comes at a price, always has and always will. That price consists of everything from taking advantage of slave labor, dumping toxic waste into our waterways, murdering those who take a stand for justice, destroying cultures, destroying environments and exploiting and oppressing anyone or anything that poses to be a threat, nuisance, or a bump along the path to riches. . . .

The ELF realizes the profit motive, caused and reinforced by the capitalist society, is destroying all life on this planet. The only way, at this point in time, to stop that continued destruction of life is to by any means necessary take the profit motive out of killing.

Using real direct action in the form of economic sabotage, the ELF is targeting what the greedy entities care about, their pocketbooks. By inflicting as much economic damage as possible, the ELF can allow a given entity to decide it is in their best economic interests to stop destroying life for the sake of profit. . . .

ELF targets

The specific target areas of the ELF are constantly increasing and will continue to grow to include any threat to life on this planet caused by greedy quests for monetary gain. The ELF targets have included such issues as deforestation (for human development of roadways, for luxurious living and/or recreation areas, for profit by selling or using trees, etc.), urban sprawl, genetic engineering, natural habitat and ecosystem destruction, the use of slave labor by corporations and more.

The most notorious action performed by the ELF in North America to date was the October 18, 1998, fires set at Vail Resorts, Inc. Vail, known as one of the premiere ski resorts in the world, had proposed an 885 acre expansion into one of the last remaining habitats for the Canadian lynx in the United States. Despite clear opposition from a vast majority of the local community and a ten year legal battle by local environmentalists, Vail was still moving forward with the expansion plans. Members of the ELF felt it was time to increase the opposition. The action caused an estimated $12–$26 million in damages to Vail and brought the issue of expansion into wilderness once again into the international spotlight. The communiqué sent by the ELF taking credit for this action appeared as follows,

---

Any entity . . . that continues to destroy the natural environment for the sake of profit and greed may be considered the next target of the group.

"On behalf of the lynx, five buildings and four ski lifts at Vail were reduced to ashes on the night of Sunday, October 18th. Vail, Inc. is already the largest ski operation in North America and now wants to expand even further. The 12 miles of roads and 885 acres of clearcuts will ruin the last, best lynx habitat in the state. Putting profits ahead of Colorado's wildlife will not be tolerated. This action is just a warning. We will be back if this greedy corporation continues to trespass into wild and unroaded areas. For your safety and convenience, we strongly advise skiers to choose other destinations until Vail cancels its inexcusable plans for expansion.—Earth Liberation Front"

On December 27, 1998, the ELF burned down the corporate headquarters of US Forest Industries in Medford, Oregon. This particular target served as the corporate headquarters for four mills; a White City veneer mill and a Grants Pass plywood mill in Oregon, a sawmill in Florida and a studmill in Colorado. The action caused an estimated $500,000–$800,000 in damages to US Forest Industries. The communiqué sent by the ELF taking credit for this action stated,

"To celebrate the holidays we decided on a bonfire. Unfortunately for U.S. Forest Industries it was at their corporate headquarters office. . . . On the foggy night after Christmas, when everyone was digesting their turkey and pie, Santa's ELFs dropped two five-gallon buckets of diesel/ unleaded mix and a gallon jug with cigarette delays; which proved to be more than enough to get this party started. This was in retribution for all the wild forests and animals lost to feed the wallets of greedy fucks like Jerry Bramwell, U.S.F.I. president . . . and it is a warning to all others responsible, we do not sleep and we won't quit."

Just under a year later, on December 25, 1999, the ELF targeted the northwest regional headquarters of Boise Cascade in Monmouth, Oregon. A $1 million fire set by the ELF burned the 8,000 square foot building to the ground. A few days after the fire the ELF sent the following communiqué,

"Boise Cascade has been very naughty. After ravaging the forests of the Pacific Northwest, Boise Cascade now looks towards the virgin forests of Chile. Early Christmas morning, elves left coal in Boise Cascade's stocking. Four buckets of diesel and gas with kitchen timer delay destroyed their regional headquarters in Monmouth, Oregon. Let this be a lesson to all greedy multinational corporations who don't respect their ecosystems. The elves are watching.—Earth Liberation Front"

Boise Cascade had recently teamed up with Maderas Condor, a Chilean company, to continue their expanding practices of deforestation in the Puerto Montt area of Chile, one of the few remaining areas in the world which had remained free from massive cutting. . . .

In addition to the actions listed above, the ELF have taken responsibility for spiking trees in Eugene, Oregon, and in Bloomington, Indiana. They have burned and caused severe economic damage to a series of homes on Long Island, New York, and torched Superior Lumber Company in Glendale, Oregon. In addition the ELF have continued on with their work against genetic engineering targeting the Delta & Pine Land Company Research Cotton Gin in Visalia, California, (a Monsanto subsidiary) and the University of Minnesota at St. Paul. More recently the ELF continued to broaden its targets with actions taken against a Nike Outlet store in Albertville, Minnesota, against an Old Navy Outlet Center on Long Island and more.

The ideology of the ELF reveals that any entity, (whether it be an individual, corporation, governmental or non-governmental agency) that continues to destroy the natural environment for the sake of profit and greed may be considered the next target of the group. . . .

Aren't the ELF targets covered by insurance?

A common argument against the actions of the ELF has been that each target has been covered by insurance so the given entity fails to suffer little if any economic loss. While it is largely true that most if not all of the ELF targets have been insured it is completely ludicrous to believe that insurance companies can suffer losses of hundreds of thousands to millions of dollars without greatly raising the rates of insurance. If the given entity or even industry was targeted repeatedly by the ELF, insurance companies would either cease to cover these entities or raise the cost too high for a profitable business.

The only problem with ELF actions at this point is there are not enough occurring.

Is the ELF a terrorist and violent organization?

Federal authorities and mainstream media particularly in the United States have done an outstanding job at feeding the public false rhetoric largely associated with the term ecoterrorism. Any action taken by the ELF has been labeled as ecoterrorist by the press and law enforcement for a particular, very conscious purpose.

What would happen if a major ELF action was taken and instead of instantly labeling it as ecoterrorism, the press and authorities did not take a biased perspective and honestly revealed the entire story including the motives for taking that action? Perhaps the public might be a little too eager to support the action and a lot less likely to quickly condemn the group. . . .

By labeling an action or a news event, the public is forced to adopt the media created stigma, either positive or negative in response to that label. Think of what goes through your mind when you hear the term terrorist. Usually it relates somehow to racist beliefs and stereotypes about Arabs, about airline hijackings, violence, and about how terrorists need to be caught and/or killed to be kept away from society. So when the federal government and the mainstream press immediately label actions of the ELF as ecoterrorism all this can do is create a negative stereotype in the minds of the public. Unfortunately as the pressures of mind control through labeling increase it becomes more difficult to allow the mind to remain open to independently process information and form less biased opinions. Which is precisely what the federal government and law enforcement want is to make sure that the mainstream public immediately equates the ELF with ecoterrorism.

> *The ELF is not an ecoterrorist organization or any sort of terrorist organization but rather one that is working to protect all life on planet earth.*

Can you imagine just what might occur if the ELF was not labeled negatively? What if people were honestly told why the group exists and who its targets are? Obviously more and more people would support and take part in ELF actions.

The ELF is not an ecoterrorist organization or any sort of terrorist organization but rather one that is working to protect all life on planet earth. It is amazingly hypocritical for mainstream media and the federal government to label the ELF as a terrorist group yet at the same time ignoring the U.S. government and U.S. based corporations which every day exploit, torture, and murder people around the world.

Why don't members use more traditional tactics?

The mainstream public has been fed an extreme amount of false and misleading propaganda in regards to "traditional tactics", those which are strictly legal and sanctioned by the state. In reality a more honest definition of traditional tactics would include illegal direct action such as economic sabotage due to its crucial role in numerous successful social and political movements throughout history.

The ELF does not engage in more traditional tactics simply because they have been proven not to work, especially on their own. The popular, modern mainstream environmental movement, which began arguably in the early 1960s, has failed in its attempts to bring about the needed protection to stop the destruction of life on this planet. This fact cannot be rightly disputed. The quality of our air, water, and soil continues to decrease as more and more life forms on the planet suffer and die as a result. How much longer are we supposed to wait to actually stop the destruction of life?

A belief in state sanctioned legal means of social change is also a sign of faith in the legal system of that same state. The ELF clearly do not have any faith in the legal system of the state when it comes to protecting life. The state has repeatedly shown itself to care far more for the protection of commerce and profits than that of its people and the natural environment. To place faith in that same state as though it will do what is in the best interests of justice and life is utter foolishness and a grave mistake. The state is a major portion of the problem.

There is also a certain intelligence and logic to the idea that with one night's work, a few individuals can accomplish what years of legal battles and millions of dollars most likely did not. . . .

Do ELF actions alienate other groups?

The members of the ELF have never stated that the tactics of their group will on their own achieve full change. Of course there needs to be public education. The ELF considers itself one part of a global movement which uses a variety of tactics to stop the destruction of life. The ELF actions on their own do not alienate the environmental movement. . . .

No one in their right mind can honestly state that the popular environmental movement using state sanctioned tactics has been successful. It is very obvious something more is needed. There is no tolerable excuse for an individual or organization that claims to be a part of the movement to protect all life on the planet to come out publicly against the actions of the ELF. If the individual or particular organization disagrees with the tactics it is just as easy to come out publicly when asked and respond with a statement such as, "although I or our organization does not take part in actions like those of the ELF, I or we can understand the motivations because the threat to life on this planet is very real and serious." What this statement does is to not publicly show a major rift in the movement but to give at least the perception of a varied movement strong and rich in diversity.

Ensuring no one is hurt

The guidelines for the ELF specifically require members to take all necessary precautions to ensure no one is physically injured. In the history of the ELF internationally no one has been injured from the group's actions and that is not a coincidence. Yes, the use of fire as a tool is dangerous but when used properly it can tremendously aid in the destruction of property associated with the killing of life. . . .

Remember the ELF exists to protect life on this planet. The choice to use economic sabotage is a very deliberate and purposeful strategy to target the real underlying threat to life—the quest for profit and power. The ELF does not engage in state sanctioned tactics or those which physically harm people or life in general due to the group's belief that economic sabotage is the best, most direct way to take the profit motive out of destroying the planet.

The real violence and danger comes from businesses clear-cutting forests and destroying ecosystems, from pollutants carelessly pumped into our air by industrial and consumer society, from water being poisoned to the point of being undrinkable, by people eating commercially grown non-organic food, and many, many more. Very often by labeling the ELF as violent it is a means by which mainstream society, government, and big business can attempt to forget about the real true violence which occurs everyday, the violence against life.

16

The Earth Liberation Front Engages in Domestic Terrorism

James F. Jarboe

James F. Jarboe is the chief of the Domestic Terrorism Section of the Counterterrorism Division of the Federal Bureau of Investigation. One of his duties is to monitor activities and investigations of radical environmental groups.

Although it is ostensibly dedicated to protecting the environment, the Earth Liberation Front (ELF) has caused more property damage than any other grassroots American political organization. While ELF activities have not yet killed anyone, their use of firebombs and other methods of sabotage puts them in the same category as domestic terrorists. The FBI views the actions of this group as dangerous and illegal and will pursue them as it does any other group dedicated to creating economic havoc in the United States.

During the past several years, special interest extremism, as characterized by the . . . Earth Liberation Front (ELF), has emerged as a serious [domestic] terrorist threat. Generally, extremist groups engage in much activity that is protected by constitutional guarantees of free speech and assembly. Law enforcement becomes involved when the volatile talk of these groups transgresses into unlawful action. The FBI estimates that the ELF have committed more than 600 criminal acts in the United States since 1996, resulting in damages in excess of 43 million dollars. . . .

Disaffected environmentalists, in 1980, formed a radical group called "Earth First!" and engaged in a series of protests and civil disobedience events. In 1984, however, members introduced "tree spiking" (insertion of metal or ceramic spikes in trees in an effort to damage saws) as a tactic to thwart logging. In 1992, the ELF was founded in Brighton, England, by Earth First! members who refused to abandon criminal acts as a tactic when others wished to mainstream Earth First! . . . In 1994, founders of the San Francisco branch of Earth First! published in *The Earth First! Jour-*

James F. Jarboe, "The Threat of Eco-Terrorism," www.fbi.gov, February 12, 2002.

nal a recommendation that Earth First! mainstream itself in the United States, leaving criminal acts other than unlawful protests to the ELF.

"Monkeywrenching"

The ELF advocates "monkeywrenching," a euphemism for acts of sabotage and property destruction against industries and other entities perceived to be damaging to the natural environment. "Monkeywrenching" includes tree spiking, arson, sabotage of logging or construction equipment, and other types of property destruction. . . .

The most destructive practice of ELF is arson. ELF members consistently use improvised incendiary devices equipped with crude but effective timing mechanisms. These incendiary devices are often constructed based upon instructions found on the ELF websites. ELF criminal incidents often involve pre-activity surveillance and well-planned operations. Members are believed to engage in significant intelligence gathering against potential targets, including the review of industry/trade publications, photographic/video surveillance of potential targets, and posting details about potential targets on the internet.

The ELF advocates "monkeywrenching," a euphemism for acts of sabotage and property destruction against industries and other entities perceived to be damaging to the natural environment.

The ELF have claimed credit for several raids including a November 1997 attack of the Bureau of Land Management wild horse corrals near Burns, Oregon, where arson destroyed the entire complex resulting in damages in excess of four hundred and fifty thousand dollars and the June 1998 arson attack of a U.S. Department of Agriculture Animal Damage Control Building near Olympia, Washington, in which damages exceeded two million dollars. The ELF claimed sole credit for the October 1998, arson of a Vail, Colorado, ski facility in which four ski lifts, a restaurant, a picnic facility and a utility building were destroyed. Damage exceeded $12 million. On 12/27/1998, the ELF claimed responsibility for the arson at the U.S. Forest Industries Office in Medford, Oregon, where damages exceeded five hundred thousand dollars. Other arsons in Oregon, New York, Washington, Michigan, and Indiana have been claimed by the ELF. Recently, the ELF has also claimed attacks on genetically engineered crops and trees. The ELF claims these attacks have totaled close to $40 million in damages. . . .

Currently, more than 26 FBI field offices have pending investigations associated with ELF activities. Despite all of our efforts (increased resources allocated, . . . successful arrests and prosecutions), law enforcement has a long way to go to adequately address the problem of eco-terrorism. Groups such as . . . the ELF present unique challenges. There is little if any hierarchal structure to such entities. Eco-terrorists are unlike traditional criminal enterprises which are often structured and organized.

Organizations to Contact

The editors have compiled the following list of organizations concerned with the issues debated in this book. The descriptions are derived from materials provided by the organizations. All have publications or information available for interested readers. The list was compiled on the date of publication of the present volume; the information provided here may change. Be aware that many organizations take several weeks or longer to respond to inquiries, so allow as much time as possible.

Alaska Forest Association (AFA)
111 Stedman St., Suite 200, Ketchikan, AK 99901
(907) 225-6114 • fax: (907) 225-5920
e-mail: afa@akforest.org • Web site: www.akforest.org

The Alaska Forest Association (AFA) is an industry trade association whose members hold business interests in the timber industry of Alaska. The AFA is committed to advancing the promotion and maintenance of a healthy forest products industry in Alaska. To do so it works to maximize public and private timber supply throughout the state and enhance private property rights. The AFA seeks to provide accurate information and education concerning forest uses and forestry products to the public and the media.

American Motorcyclist Association (AMA)
13515 Yarmouth Dr., Pickering, OH 43147
(614) 856-1900 • fax: (614) 856-1920
e-mail: ama@ama-cycle.org • Web site: www.ama-cycle.org

The American Motorcyclist Association is an organization with a history of pursuing, protecting, and promoting the interests of motorcycle enthusiasts. With more than 250,000 members, the AMA defends motorcyclists' rights in the United States by opposing antimotorcycling discrimination at the local, state, federal, and corporate levels.

Americans for Responsible Recreational Access (ARRA)
e-mail: webmaster@mail.arra-access.com
Web site: www.arra-access.com/arra/home.html

Americans for Responsible Recreational Access (ARRA) is a pro–off-road vehicle organization that seeks to protect Americans' right to responsibly experience and enjoy the public lands that belong to the citizens of the United States. The members of ARRA, which include horseback riders, personal watercraft users, and off-highway vehicle and snowmobile riders, have joined together to provide input on decisions regarding land use designation, recreation opportunities, and preservation.

Campaign for America's Wilderness
122 C St. NW, Suite 240, Washington, DC 20001
(202) 544-3691 • fax: (202) 544-5197
e-mail: Marcia Argust, Washington representative, margust@leaveitwild.org
Web site: www.leaveitwild.org

The Campaign for America's Wilderness is a national effort to permanently protect the nation's last wildlands by placing them into the National Wilderness Preservation System, where they will remain in a natural state for the use and enjoyment of future generations. The organization participates in campaigns of state coalitions and citizen groups across the country to raise awareness of wilderness issues and to seek adoption of proposals and initiatives that will save the remaining wilderness.

Center for Biological Diversity
PO Box 710, Tucson, AZ 85702-0710
(520) 623-5252 • fax: (520) 623-9797
e-mail: center@biologicaldiversity.org
Web site: www.sw-center.org/swcbd/index.html

The Center for Biological Diversity believes that the health and vigor of human societies and the integrity and wildness of the natural environment are closely linked. Combining conservation biology with litigation and policy advocacy, the Center for Biological Diversity seeks to protect animals and plants threatened by extinction, the wilderness they need to survive, and by extension the spiritual welfare of generations to come.

Competitive Enterprise Institute (CEI)
1001 Connecticut Ave. NW, Suite 1250, Washington, DC 20036
(202) 331-1010 • fax: (202) 331-0640
e-mail: info@cei.org • Web site: www.cei.org

CEI encourages the use of the free market and private property rights to protect the environment. It advocates removing governmental regulatory barriers and establishing a system in which the private sector would be responsible for the environment. CEI's publications include the monthly newsletter *CEI Update* and editorials in its On Point series, such as "Property Owners Deserve Equal Access to Justice."

Environmental Defense Fund (EDF)
257 Park Ave. S., New York, NY 10010
(212) 505-2100 • fax: (212) 505-0892
e-mail: members@environmentaldefense.org • Web site: www.edf.org

The fund is a public interest organization of lawyers, scientists, and economists dedicated to the protection and improvement of environmental quality and public health. It publishes brochures, fact sheets, and the bimonthly *EDF Letter*.

Forest Service Employees for Environmental Ethics (FSEEE)
PO Box 11615, Eugene, OR 97440
(541) 484-2692 • fax: (541) 484-3004
e-mail: fseee@fseee.org • Web site: www.fseee.org

FSEEE is made up of thousands of concerned citizens; present, former, and retired Forest Service employees; other government resource managers, and activists working to change the Forest Service's basic land management philosophy. It seeks to forge a socially responsible value system for the Forest Service based on a land ethic that ensures ecologically and economically sustainable resource management. FSEEE believes that the land is a public trust to be passed with reverence from generation to generation.

The Foundation for National Progress
731 Market St., Suite 600, San Francisco, CA 94103
(415) 665-6637 • fax: (415) 665-6696
e-mail: backtalk@motherjones.com • Web site: www.motherjones.com

The Foundation for National Progress is an independent nonprofit organization affiliated with *Mother Jones* magazine. It seeks to promote social justice by means of quality investigative reporting. It publishes *Mother Jones* magazine.

Foundation for Research on Economics and the Environment (FREE)
945 Technology Blvd., Suite 101F, Bozeman, MT 59718
(406) 585-1776 • fax: (406) 585-3000
e-mail: free@mcn.net • Web site: www.free-eco.org

FREE is a research and education foundation committed to freedom, environmental quality, and economic progress. It works to reform environmental policy by using the principles of private property rights, the free market, and the rule of law. FREE publishes the quarterly newsletter *FREE Perspectives on Economics and the Environment* and produces a biweekly syndicated op-ed column.

Greenpeace USA
702 H St. NW, Suite 300, Washington DC 20001
(202) 462-1177 • fax: (202) 462-4507
e-mail: greenpeace.usa@wdc.greenpeace.org
Web site: www.greenpeace.org/international_en

Greenpeace has been campaigning against environmental degradation since 1971. It seeks to expose environmental criminals and to challenge government and corporations when they fail to live up to their mandate to safeguard the environment. The organization uses research, lobbying, and diplomacy to pursue its goals, as well as high-profile, nonviolent conflict to raise the level of public debate.

The Heritage Foundation
214 Massachusetts Ave. NE, Washington, DC 20002
(800) 544-4843 • fax: (202) 544-2260
e-mail: pubs@heritage.org • Web site: www.heritage.org

The Heritage Foundation is a conservative think tank that supports the principles of free enterprise and limited government in environmental matters. Its many publications include the following position papers: "Can No One Stop the EPA?" "How to Talk About Property Rights: Why Protecting Property Rights Benefits All Americans," and "How to Help the Environment Without Destroying Jobs."

Independent Petroleum Association of America
1201 Fifteenth St. NW, Suite 300, Washington, DC 20005
(202) 857-4722 • fax: (202) 857-4799
Web site: www.ipaa.org

The Independent Petroleum Association of America is a trade organization that represents the interests of America's oil and natural gas producers. It advocates its members' views before Congress, the administration, and federal agencies. It publishes the weekly newsletter *IPAA Washington Report*.

The Mercatus Center at George Mason University
3301 N. Fairfax Dr., Suite 450, Arlington, VA 22201
(800) 815-5711 • fax: (703) 993-4935
e-mail: mercatus@gmu.edu • Web site: www.mercatus.org

The Mercatus Center at George Mason University is a conservative research and education center. It supports scholarship that investigates how government regulations affect commerce and publishes papers and editorials to disseminate that information.

National Audubon Society
700 Broadway, New York, NY 10003
(212) 979-3000 • fax: (212) 979-3188
e-mail: education@audubon.org • Web site: www.audubon.org

Audubon's mission is to conserve and restore natural ecosystems, focusing on birds, other wildlife, and their habitats for the benefit of humanity and Earth's biological diversity. It consists of a national network of community-based nature centers and chapters, scientific and educational programs, and advocacy on behalf of areas sustaining important bird populations.

National Off-Highway Vehicle Conservation Council
4718 S. Taylor Dr., Sheboygan, WI 53081-3362
(800) 348-6487 • fax: (920) 458-3446
e-mail: trailhead@nohvcc.org

The National Off-Highway Vehicle Conservation Council is a publicly supported education foundation organized for the sole purpose of promoting safe, responsible, family oriented off-highway recreational experiences. It is a forum for organizations and supporters of OHV recreation, including OHV manufacturers, dealers, clubs, and enthusiasts.

Natural Resources Defense Council (NRDC)
40 W. Twentieth St., New York, NY 10011
(212) 727-2700 • fax: (212) 727-1773
e-mail: nrdcinfo@nrdc.org • Web site: www.nrdc.org/default.asp

Natural Resources Defense Council (NRDC) is an environmental action organization. It uses law, science, and the support of members and online activists to protect the planet's wildlife and wild places and to ensure a safe and healthy environment for all living things. The NRDC works to protect the quality of the air, land, and water and to defend endangered natural places.

Political Economy Research Center (PERC)
502 S. Nineteenth Ave., Suite 211, Bozeman, MT 59718-6872
(406) 587-9591 • fax: (406) 586-7555
e-mail: perc@perc.org • Web site: www.perc.org

PERC is a research and education foundation that focuses primarily on environmental and natural resource issues. It emphasizes the advantages of free markets and the importance of private property rights in environmental protection. PERC's publications include the monthly *PERC Reports* and papers in the PERC Policy Series, such as "The Common Law: How It Protects the Environment."

Sierra Club
85 Second St., Second Fl., San Francisco, CA 94105-3441
(415) 977-5500 • fax: (415) 977-5799
e-mail: information@sierraclub.org • Web site: www.sierraclub.org

The Sierra Club is a nonprofit public interest organization that promotes conservation of the natural environment by influencing public policy decisions—legislative, administrative, legal, and electoral. It publishes *Sierra* magazine as well as books on the environment.

The Southeast Alaska Conservation Council (SEACC)
419 Sixth St., Suite 200, Juneau, AK 99801
(907) 586-6942
e-mail: info@seacc.org • Web site: www.seacc.org

The Southeast Alaska Conservation Council (SEACC) is a coalition of eighteen volunteer conservation groups in fourteen southeast Alaskan communities surrounded by the Tongass National Forest. SEACC's members include small-scale wood product manufacturers, commercial fishermen, Native Alaskans, sportsmen and women, and others who want to safeguard the Tongass's environment while providing for the sustainable use of the region's resources.

U.S. Department of Energy
1000 Independence Ave. SW, Washington, DC 20585
(800) DIAL-DOE • fax: (202) 586-4403
Web site: www.doe.gov

The Department of Energy is an agency of the federal government whose mission is to advance the national, economic, and energy security of the United States; to promote scientific and technological innovation in support of that mission; and to ensure the environmental cleanup of the national nuclear weapons complex.

U.S. Environmental Protection Agency (EPA)
401 M St. SW, Washington, DC 20460
(202) 260-2090
Web site: www.epa.gov

The EPA is the government agency charged with protecting human health and safeguarding the natural environment. It works to protect Americans from environmental health risks, enforce federal environmental regulations, and ensure that environmental protection is an integral consideration in U.S. policy. The EPA publishes many reports, fact sheets, and educational materials.

U.S. Fish and Wildlife Service
1250 Twenty-Fifth St. NW, Washington, DC 20037
(202) 293-4800
Web site: www.fws.gov

The U.S. Fish and Wildlife Service is a network of regional offices, national wildlife refuges, research and development centers, national fish hatcheries, and wildlife law enforcement agents. The service's primary goal is to conserve, protect, and enhance fish and wildlife and their habitats. It publishes an endangered species list as well as fact sheets, pamphlets, and information on the Endangered Species Act.

U.S. PIRG
218 D St. SE, Washington, DC 20003
(202) 546-9707 • fax: (202) 546-2461
e-mail: webmaster@pirg.org • Web site: http://uspirg.org

PIRGs are Public Interest Research Groups that act as watchdogs for the public interest in all fifty states. U.S. PIRG was created by state PIRGs to give a unique "outside the beltway" perspective and provide the grassroots power necessary to influence the national policy debate in order to protect the environment, encourage a fair, sustainable economy, and foster responsive, democratic government.

Wilderness Land Trust
PO Box 1420, Carbondale, CO 81623
(970) 963-1725
e-mail: reid@wildernesslandtrust.org • Web site: www.wildernesslandtrust.org

The Wilderness Land Trust acquires private lands in federally designated wilderness areas and transfers them to public ownership in order to preserve them in their natural state. The organization works cooperatively with the U.S. Forest Service and the Bureau of Land Management to identify land acquisition opportunities, obtain congressional appropriations, and transfer wilderness parcels to public ownership.

The Wilderness Society
1615 M St. NW, Washington, DC 20036
(800) 843-9453
e-mail: member@tws.org • Web site: www.wilderness.org

The Wilderness Society uses specific expertise, analysis, and advocacy to protect and restore America's wilderness areas. Programs include protecting the Arctic Wildlife Refuge from oil and gas drilling; staving off logging and road building on 58 million acres of roadless lands; curbing the abuse of lands by off-road vehicle users; and protecting wild places within the lower forty-eight states from oil development.

Wilderness Watch
PO Box 9175, Missoula, MT 59807
(406) 542-2048 • fax: (406) 542-7714
e-mail: wild@wildernesswatch.org • Web site: www.wildernesswatch.org

Founded in 1989, Wilderness Watch is the only national organization whose sole focus is the preservation and proper stewardship of lands and rivers already included in the National Wilderness Preservation System and National Wild and Scenic Rivers System. The organization grew out of the concern that while much emphasis is being placed on adding new areas to these systems, the conditions of existing wilderness and rivers are largely being ignored. The organization fights to ensure the stewardship of these wild places through independent citizen oversight, education, and the monitoring of federal management activities.

Worldwatch Institute
1776 Massachusetts Ave. NW, Washington, DC 20036-1904
(202) 452-1999 • fax: (202) 296-7365
e-mail: worldwatch@worldwatch.org • Web site: www.worldwatch.org

Worldwatch is a research organization that analyzes and calls attention to global problems, including environmental concerns such as the loss of cropland, forests, habitat, species, and water supplies. It compiles the annual *State of the World* and *Vital Signs* anthologies and publishes the bimonthly *Worldwatch* magazine as well as papers in the Environmental Alert series, such as "Fighting for Survival: Environmental Decline, Social Conflict, and the New Age of Insecurity."

Bibliography

Books

Terry L. Anderson

Political Environmentalism: Going Behind the Green Curtain. Stanford, CA: Hoover Institution Press, 2000.

Lloyd Burton

Worship and Wilderness: Culture, Religion, and Law in Public Lands. Madison: University of Wisconsin Press, 2002.

Tim Butler, ed.

Wild Earth: Wild Ideas for a World Out of Balance. Minneapolis: Milkweed Editions, 2002.

Frank Friedman

Practical Guide to Environmental Management. Washington, DC: Environmental Law Institute, 1995.

J.W. Handmer, T.W. Norton, and S.R. Dovers, eds.

Ecology, Uncertainty and Policy: Managing Ecosystems for Sustainability. New York: Pearson Education, 2001.

Ted Kerasote, ed.

Return of the Wild: The Future of Our Natural Lands. Washington, DC: Island Press, 2001.

Andro Linklater

Measuring America: How an Untamed Wilderness Shaped the United States and Fulfilled the Promise of Democracy. New York: Walker, 2002.

Bob R. O'Brien

Our National Parks and the Search for Sustainability. Austin: University of Texas Press, 1999.

Rosemary O'Leary

Managing for the Environment: Understanding the Legal, Organizational, and Policy Challenges. San Francisco: Jossey-Bass, 1999.

Diana Wege

Land America Leaves Wild. Washington, DC: Wilderness Society, 2000.

Frank Wheat

California Desert Miracle: The Fight for Desert Parks and Wilderness. San Diego: Sunbelt, 1999.

Bill Willers

Unmanaged Landscapes: Voices for Untamed Nature. Washington, DC: Island Press, 1999.

Periodicals

Kera Abraham

"Rough and Ready for Mining?" *Forest Magazine*, Winter 2003.

John Balzar

"Ah, Sweet Nature . . . but Only If You Can Afford a Piece of It; Please Save Some for Us, Mr. President," *Los Angeles Times*, August 18, 2002.

Rick Bass

"The Right to Be Wild," *Mother Jones*, November/December 2003.

Mark Blaine	"Mud Money," *Forest Magazine*, Summer 2002.
Jennifer Bogo	"The Hottest Spot," *Audubon*, December 2003.
John Chaffey	"Wilderness and Its Management," *Geography Review*, November 1999.
Alexander Cockburn	"Wilderness Society: The Saga of Shame Continues," *Nation*, March 6, 1995.
William Cronon	"This Land Is Your Land: Turning to Nature in a Time of Crisis," *Audubon*, January 2002.
Joseph P. Flood	"Focus Groups Improve Wilderness Management Efforts," *Parks & Recreation*, May 2002.
Clare Ginger	"Discourse and Argument in Bureau of Land Management Wilderness Environmental Impact Statements," *Policy Studies*, Summer 2000.
Jennifer Hattam	"Highway Robbery: Make-Believe Roads Threaten Real Wilderness," *Sierra*, July/August 2003.
Jocelyn Kaiser	"Bringing Science to the National Parks," *Science*, April 7, 2000.
Paul R. Krausman and Brian Czech	"Wildlife Management Activities in Wilderness Areas in the Southwestern United States," *Wildlife Society Bulletin*, Fall 2000.
John G. Mitchell	"Our Great Estate," *Sierra*, March/April 2004.
Robert H. Nelson	"Scorched-Earth Policies," *Wall Street Journal*, November 3, 2003.
George Nickas	"Preserving an Enduring Wilderness: Challenges and Threats to the National Wilderness Preservation System," *Denver University Law Review*, Winter 1999.
Matt Rasmussen	"Wildlife Watchers: The Big Business of Loving Wildlife in Alaska," *Forest Magazine*, Spring 2002.
James M. Ridenour	"Confronting the Crisis in Our National Parks," *USA Today Magazine*, September 1997.
Robert J. Smith	"A New Beginning for Our Forests," *San Diego Union-Tribune*, December 9, 2003.
Liz Thomas	"Dealing with Wilderness," *Journal of Land, Resources and Environmental Law*, Fall 2001.
Sandra B. Zellmer	"The Roadless Area Controversy: Past, Present, and Future," *Rocky Mountain Mineral Law Institute*, Annual 2002.

Internet Sources

Diane Alden	"Broken Promise Land," NewsMax.com, January 30, 2001. www.newsmax.com/commentmax/print.shtml?a=2001/1/30/034124.
Marego Athans	"Timber, Tourism Set Sights on Tongass Forest," Sunspot.net, May 9, 2001. www.sunspot.net/news/nationworld/balte.alaska09may09,0,1245446story.

Index